BREATHE ME

ALSO BY GENEVA LEE

THE RIVALS SAGA
Blacklist
Backlash
Bombshell

THE ROYALS SAGA
Command Me
Conquer Me
Crown Me
Crave Me
Covet Me
Capture Me
Complete Me
Cross Me
Claim Me
Consume Me
Breathe Me
Break Me

THE SINNERS SAGA
Beautiful Criminal
Beautiful Sinner
Beautiful Forever

The Sins That Bind Us

THE ROYALS SAGA: ELEVEN

BREATHE ME

GENEVA LEE

IVY ESTATE
SEATTLE

BREATHE ME

Copyright © 2020 by Geneva Lee.

All rights reserved.

This book or any portion thereof may not be reproduced or used in any manner whatsoever without the express written permission of the publisher except for the use of brief quotations in a book review.

This is a work of fiction. Names, characters, businesses, places, events and incidents are either the products of the author's imagination or used in a fictitious manner. Any resemblance to actual persons, living or dead, or actual events is purely coincidental.

Ivy Estate Publishing + Media

www.GenevaLee.com

First published, 2020.

Cover design © Date Book Designs.

Image © Andrey Kiselev/Adobe Stock.

*To those who are fighting
for themselves,
for others,
for love:
never give up.*

1

SMITH

The path to hell was paved with remodeling dust. I stepped over a precariously abandoned wood saw and made my way past two men arguing over grout for the backsplash. If I wasn't careful I would be drawn into the sodding debate. I'd had enough arguing in my ten years as a lawyer to know that some battles aren't worth fighting, particularly when it came to tiles. I only had one thing on my mind—one person, actually—and I didn't care to speak to anyone before I saw her. It never sat well to leave my wife, Belle, alone with an entire construction crew for the day. First, she had a tendency to add more work to the project, which was already well-past due, but, mostly, because I coveted her. It wasn't that I didn't trust her. It was that I wanted her all to myself. The last few days I'd had to share her with ten crew members, a foreman, and the rest of the household staff. Gone were the honeymoon days of fucking her two steps into the entryway of our London townhouse. I knew that when I pushed to move to the country. I just hadn't expected that finding her in all the chaos would be as daunting as finding a moment alone.

For five months, we'd sought the perfect estate to call home, butting heads at every turn. Our wishlist had turned out to be a collection of opposite needs and wants. She wanted a homey feel. I wanted a modern kitchen. She insisted on a swimming pool. I hated them. She wanted to be within an hour's drive of London or less. I wanted to take her as far from that city as possible. I'd never voiced that particular desire out of a well-honed sense of self-preservation. I had no doubt Belle suspected that I wanted her away from not only the city's chaos but also her circle of friends. I loved them like an extended family almost as much as she did, but being best friends with the monarchy meant having a target on our backs. It was time for a new chapter. We'd agreed on that much if we argued about everything else.

The only option, in the end, had been to buy something that checked as many boxes as possible and rip apart what didn't work. Thornham Park had been built in the late sixteenth century, updated every few decades to include the latest conveniences like plumbing and electricity as well as the passing whims of its various owners. Its location in Sussex might not have been far enough from London for my liking, but it had everything else she wanted, meaning it would fulfill the only item I saw as non-negotiable: moving out of London.

As it turned out, five months of fighting with a hormonal, pregnant woman paled in comparison to dealing with contractors. I began to suspect this was part of her plan the whole time. As long as half the house was in ruins, we kept finding ourselves back at our home in Holland Park.

A quick search of the grounds yielded no results. I wouldn't have blamed Belle for trying to get away from the house, given the persistent cacophony of drills, hammers, and saws billowing from the kitchen. The remodel was nearly complete, but it would be months before we'd finished updating the entire estate. Our focus had been on the most important elements of our home: our bedroom and bath, the kitchen and living areas, and, of course, the nursery. We'd been coming back and forth the last few weeks. Belle had been taking her goddaughter, Elizabeth, a couple days a week to help her best friend out, and I'd been wrapping up the last of our affairs in London. With the baby due any day, I'd finally convinced her to move the bulk of her belongings here. Now, I just had to convince her to stay put more than an evening at a time.

Twenty minutes later, I had no choice but to check my least favorite amenity of our new home: the pool. It has felt like a cosmic joke to finally find the perfect country house within a short drive to London—Belle's demand—but with the security features I'd insisted upon, only to discover it came with a sodding pool in its basement. The coincidence left a bad taste in my mouth. My family's home in Kensington, the house I'd grown up in after leaving Scotland when my father took a job in England, had also had a pool in its basement. My memories of that pool were colored by the memory of finding his body in it. I'd been pleased to get rid of the old albatross and move to Holland Park with her after we married. I'd never expected that I'd finally find the ideal estate and it would have the same feature. Even without the grim memories of my childhood home, I didn't particularly love the idea, especially with a baby on the way, but I couldn't deny the estate was otherwise a perfect match.

Stepping into the muggy lower level, I spotted her. She was doing a lap. The water rippled around her, her shapely ass cresting over its surface to put on a private show for me. And it was a show, because Belle wasn't wearing a stitch of clothing. I had a house full of contractors and their crews, and she was down here skinny-dipping. I felt a familiar swell of blood in my groin. No matter how many times I saw her, how many times I fucked her, how many times I made love to her, it was always the same. I only wanted more.

She reached the tiled wall at the far side of the pool and grabbed its edge. Beads of water snaked down her back as she shook her wet hair.

"Are you just going to keep watching me, pervert?" She called in a lofty voice, not bothering to turn around.

"I'm appreciating my prize possession." I wouldn't apologize for appreciating my wife. Not to her or anyone else. She was every fantasy I'd ever had, come to life.

Belle finally threw a simpering grin over her shoulder, as though she knew exactly what I was thinking, before turning to give me a full frontal view of all of her assets. Her breasts, once small and pert had rounded into globes with dark nipples that begged to be in my mouth. I reached down to adjust my dick, allowing my gaze to wander below the water's surface to the curve of her stomach where our child grew. She'd always been as lovely as her name implied, but now she was the most fucking beautiful woman on the planet.

"If looks could knock a girl up," she teased, before adding, "Oh wait."

Her hand reached to stroke her bump, and she winked at me.

"Come here." I curled my index finger, beckoning her closer. "There's something I want to show you."

"I think I can see it from here," she said dryly, but her teeth sank into her lower lip.

I glanced down at my trousers with a grin. "What a dirty mind you have, Mrs. Price."

"What a giant cock you have, Mr. Price," she purred.

"How can you tell from over there?" I reached for the towel she'd left on the chaise lounge and held it up. "Don't make me ask twice, beautiful."

Even from a distance I saw the tremble of anticipation roll through her. A familiar plan played across her face. I'd asked her to join me. She'd resisted. I'd warned her. We both knew what came next.

Belle didn't budge.

"Beautiful," I growled.

She enjoyed pressing my buttons almost as much as she enjoyed being reprimanded. It was our own brand of foreplay.

"I really should get out," she said with a sigh. "I think we have more interviews this afternoon."

I frowned at the reminder. I remained unconvinced that a nanny would be necessary. We'd gone back and forth on the issue. Trusting someone that close to our child didn't sit well with me. But neither of us could commit to being full-time caregivers. Belle planned to expand Bless, her couture wardrobe rental start-up, into a separate clothing subscription for babies. Her business partner had recently flaked on her to babysit our most recent headache, the bastard brother of King Alexander. I planned to set up a law office in the village, which would look perfectly respectable and give me an excuse to avoid future investigations on behalf of the crown. It was time for us to focus on ourselves and our family, and we were going to have our hands full. But I'd seen too much in the past few years—in a lifetime really—to believe it could be that simple.

I didn't trust easily, and I had a good reason. I couldn't imagine finding someone who would assuage my doubt.

"You're worrying," Belle interrupted my thoughts, finally gliding across the water to the entrance steps. She climbed them slowly, her long fingers clinging to the railing carefully. Each stair brought more of her sumptuous body into view and pushed my concerns farther from my mind.

"Not anymore," I promised, flicking my tongue across my lower lip. "Now, I'm just deciding what to do to you first."

"I didn't do as you told me," she pointed out with a wicked glint in her blue eyes that told me I'd been right that she wanted to be punished.

I wrapped the towel around her shoulders and brought it to cover her.

"What am I going to do with you, beautiful?" I asked, tugging the terrycloth that trapped her until she was as close as her pregnant body would allow.

Belle's head tipped back, her hair dripping across her shoulders, and smiled. "Anything you want."

In that case, we wouldn't be needing the towel. I rubbed it across her bare skin until she was dry. Pausing to study her for a moment. "Are you cold?"

"No." But she shivered.

I raised an eyebrow.

"Maybe a little," she admitted.

I slid my hand down between her thighs, coaxing her stance a little wider in the process, so I could massage my palm against her slick skin. "I can warm you up."

"But I disobeyed you," she murmured, wriggling in an

attempt to achieve more contact.

My palm twitched at the invitation. Leaning down, I drew my lips across hers, moving to trail them across her jawline until I reached her ear. "I never said I wasn't going to punish you. You'll find parts of you very warm soon."

A hesitant cough broke the spell between us, and I whipped around, placing myself between my wife and the intruder.

"Begging your pardon." Humphrey, our new butler, studiously looked away from us. His face, slightly crimson, was as sharp and angular as the tails he wore, their jet black fabric faded with age. "You have a guest. I saw her to the east drawing room. I assumed with the construction in the kitchen—"

"Thank you," I cut him off. "We'll be right up."

"I will have some tea delivered," he suggested mildly, his eyes still glued to the floor.

After this, I was going to need whiskey. Humphrey bowed before turning to wind his way up the creaky stairs to the main floor of the house.

"We're never going to have any bloody privacy," I grumbled.

"Whose idea was it to leave London for the country?" Belle reminded me, stepping away while adjusting her towel to cover herself completely.

"I want a fresh start," I said, reminding myself the same. Away from London. Away from the busy city. But, mostly, I wanted to leave our ghosts behind. After everything that had happened to us, Belle had agreed. She was more reluctant, but, fortunately, I had many methods of persuasion at my disposal—if only we could get a moment alone.

"Shall we go meet Mary Poppins?" Belle held out her hand, drawing me back to what this was really about: our future. Hers, mine, and our daughter's.

I'd get used to the household staff, and they'd get used to finding us like this.

"Lead the way, beautiful." I took her hand and guided her toward the lift. We stepped inside it, and I pressed the button for the second floor. "I'll go down and say hello. Join us when you're dressed."

When we reached the second floor, Belle stepped into the hall before turning to place a hand to stop the lift doors from sliding closed. "We're doing the right thing, aren't we? Coming here?"

I only heard the question she was really asking: Can we leave the past behind?

I smiled, and then I did something I rarely felt the need to do with my wife, I lied. "Yes. Everything is going to be simpler here. You'll see."

She nodded as I leaned across the threshold to kiss her, but her body remained rigid. That's when I realized two things: she knew it was a lie, but she'd been hoping she could believe it.

"I'll be down in a few minutes," she promised.

She disappeared from sight as the doors slid closed. I'd promised to protect her, and I'd nearly given my life to do so. Nothing would change that, but soon I would have two of them to guard. It would be easier to do that here, away from the chaos that surrounded our Royal circle of friends.

I'd prove it to her. Or I'd make it my mission to keep her so distracted that she didn't care. I was going to make this work. One way or the other.

2

BELLE

The antique lift delivered me to the first floor of the house, or as I liked to think of it: sanctuary. As soon as I stepped from the confined compartment into the corridor, the sounds of construction greeted me. Hammering, sawing—and god knows what else—rose through the landing of the stairs from the work being down on the ground level. I padded down the hall, into the east wing and slammed the bedroom door closed behind me. For a moment, I sank against the wood, clutching the towel tightly around my body. It wasn't as though living in a beautiful house on a large estate was a hardship. I'd grown up on one, save for the times I was away at boarding school. I knew what it took to run the grounds. I knew my husband's insistence on hiring a butler, a cook, a groundskeeper, and a housekeeper were all wise decisions. He'd seen to everything—almost everything.

At the moment, it was hard to imagine how quiet this house would soon be. But once the foreman and his crews finished their work, it would just be the two of us and a bunch of strangers. The nearest neighbor was several kilometers away and the village was over a fifteen minute drive. I should have expected as much when Smith said he wanted somewhere peaceful to raise our daughter. I should have been ecstatic at the prospect of living here and raising a family. I'd wanted that: to have children with Smith. I still wanted it, but I couldn't help worrying about how much I was giving up in the process. I'd nearly suggested looking for a house closer to my mother, just to know I would be near someone I knew. Thankfully, the ongoing drama surrounding my own family estate had shown me enough to know that was a bad idea.

"Chin up, soldier," I muttered to myself. Tossing the towel on the bed on my way to the master bath, I started the shower, reminding myself that it was one of the many reasons this house was going to be worth the sacrifice. The entire bathroom had been gutted, plumbing and fixtures updated, into a loo worthy of a five star resort. Smith insisted it be exactly to my standards, so that I would have a place to escape during the rest of the remodel as well as a quiet spot to relax after the baby was born. I'd opted for Carrara marble, knowing its simple sophistication would never go out of style. A two-person soaking tub overlooked the sweeping hills behind the house. His and her vessel sinks sat opposite one another on a long vanity, lit overhead by a matching set of chandeliers. The marble flooring extended to cover one wall entirely in the delicate white tile to make a massive, walk-in shower. A single pane of clear glass rose from the floor and other than two large, rainfall-style showerheads and a central drain, there was little else to the shower. It had been a trick to figure out where to put the soap so as not to spoil the effect. In the end, a small shelf had been built into the wall, allowing a place for us to stash our necessities. I'd designed the space so Smith and I could shower at the same time. Although, considering how regularly he joined me on my side of the shower, it could have been half the size.

I piled up my hair and stepped into the shower, hoping it would wash away my anxieties before going to meet with the potential nannies—another concession I'd made to my protective husband. We both had businesses to run. I'd debated selling my half of Bless, my couture clothing rental service, to my business partner, but I couldn't quite let it go. As much as I wanted to be a mummy, I didn't want to completely give up my identity. A sharp kick inside me stole my breath as though my darling girl already had opinions of her own on these matters.

"You could just come to work with me," I cooed, rubbing a circle over my ever-larger belly and earning another kick. "Us girls have to stick together."

I just didn't see why I couldn't do both: be a mum and a business woman. My best friend managed to be a mother and the Queen of England.

"With a household staff," I reminded myself with a sigh, shutting off the water. Even Clara had a nanny in the beginning. I'd been helping her since William was born. Women needed women. It didn't make me a bad future mum to have a hand and it didn't make me a bad entrepreneur to have a baby. Balance was an illusion, anyway. I'd learned that much my first year running my own company.

My wandering thoughts had resulted in too much water spraying on my hair to put it back down, and I had no time to dry it. Rearranging it into a top-knot, I popped into my closet, grabbed a blue silk scarf and tied it artfully around my head. I'd kept most of my maternity dresses in London, where I needed them for business meetings and going to the palace. In the country, I generally opted for a more comfortable wardrobe that allowed me to easily climb around construction materials, wade through the tall grass behind the estate, or lounge around after the crews left for the day. But today, I wanted to make an impression and coveralls and jumpers wouldn't do the trick. Grabbing a stretchy pair of cropped black leggings, I tugged them on, barely maintaining my balance as I pulled their high waist up and over my swollen stomach. The more pregnant I got, the harder it became to do the simplest tasks. Abandoning my side of the closet, I walked to Smith's and found a simple white Oxford. I tugged it on, buttoned the first few buttons and then tied the rest just over the waistband of the leggings. I slid on a pair of velvet Birdies, the greatest thing to happen to my feet in the last three months, and decided that was enough. It was better than showing up in sweatpants anyway.

I grabbed my phone from the nightstand and started toward the stairs, pausing when I saw a text notification.

Clara: When are you coming home? Maybe we can all have lunch?

I took a deep breath, uncertain how to respond. By all, she meant me and Edward. Lunch with Clara meant going to Buckingham. She had a newborn and there was no way around it. I happened to know that Edward missed her and would love to have lunch and see his new nephew. But Buckingham also meant Alexander, and no matter how much Edward loved his sister-in-law and friend, nothing would convince him to step foot inside that place. Nothing had for weeks. I couldn't blame him for that. I'd stopped asking him when he was going to talk with his brother out of fear that he would cut me out of his life as well. Someone had to keep an eye on him.

I responded that I'd have to check, knowing full-well that I was simply putting off a harder conversation for an easier answer now. I scrolled through my messages to see if Edward had responded to my last friendly hello, asking if he wanted to talk. I'd got back a two word response.

I'm fine.

Fine. It's all I ever got from him now. Fine? *Bollocks.* He was not fine. Not by a long shot. Who would be after the death of his husband? Especially given what had happened. He'd begun taking off on last minute trips as though he could run away from his problems. I never knew when he was in London let alone England, and Clara expected to get updates through me about his whereabouts. I hated feeling caught in the middle between my best friends. I hated being stuck out here and unable to force the two of them to finally face one another. I suspected that I just hated feeling like my real life was an hour away in the middle of London.

I turned the volume down on my ringer as I descended the last stair and braced myself. The door to the sitting room was open and I stepped inside, closing it behind me to drown out some of the construction noise.

Smith paused mid-sentence and turned to look at me, his eyes raking across me in a way that always sent a shiver racing down my spine. Even now, in the middle of one of the most mundane tasks ever—a job interview—hunger reflected in his green irises. He looked as he always did: like he was about to pounce and pin me to the wall.

Under that gaze, I felt like I always did: like I wanted him to do just that.

My husband was more than most men dreamed of being. There was handsome, and then there was Smith. Dark hair, just a shade past auburn and sharp, chiseled features formed him into more god than man. Broad shoulders that crowned a muscular upper body, he oozed with a natural arrogance that I couldn't resist. I'd tried once, after he'd hired me to be his assistant. In all fairness, I'd stayed out of his bed much longer than anyone expected. Knowing him now, I wish I hadn't waited so long. There were few vices in life more delicious than being completely owned and possessed by a man as powerful and certain as Smith Price. I hated the idea that I'd lose even a moment of them to my own stubborn willfulness. Even now, I had half a mind to drag him away to bed—or the nearest flat surface.

But we had a guest and judging from the way her incredibly thin lips had formed a straight, flat line, she disapproved of...from the looks of it, everything. The rest of her was equally sharp from the beak-like nose to her tightly pulled back hair. I forced a warm smile on my lips and strode over, hand extended.

"This is my wife, Belle," Smith introduced me, and the potential nanny gripped my hand so firmly I thought it might snap off. "Belle, meet Martha."

"It's a pleasure," I said smoothly, earning me nothing more than a grunt before she returned her attention to Smith. I took the seat next to my husband on the sofa.

"And the hours?" she asked, ignoring me entirely.

"We haven't quite decided on that." He glanced at me for confirmation.

"We only need someone part-time," I told her. "After she's born and we've been home for a while and settled in."

"You don't want part-time," she said—not to me, but Smith.

Oh hell no. A hand fell on my knee and squeezed. A warning from Smith not to get too riled up. Could he sense that I felt left out of the equation?

"We don't?" he asked politely. I'd heard him use this voice before. He reserved it for small talk.

"Consistency is key. It will be several years before the child can go off to school, but structure is essential. You're both business owners. Neither of you can commit to being the primary caregiver," she said, nailing the situation a bit too precisely for comfort. "Someone must be around to make certain discipline and structure are strictly enforced."

"I don't think babies require discipline," I blurted out before I could stop myself. Did she think she was being asked to run a nursery or a boot camp?

Martha's withering glare suggested she felt differently.

"It's certainly something to keep in mind," Smith mused, squeezing my knee twice, our secret code for *let me handle this*. "As you can see, we're still figuring out the best fit, and we will have a while before we need someone here."

"There are always preparations to be made," Martha said.

"Naturally, but we'll want to wait for construction to finish, regardless." Smith seamlessly transitioned the excuse from reason to another. "We'll be in touch."

We all rose and Smith showed her out of the room. When he returned, my eyebrow was etched into a question mark.

"Where did you find that battleaxe? I thought their type had gone extinct."

"I think they were all simply banished to the countryside," he said wearily. "Ready for round two?"

"Do you think they'll all be like her?" I asked, wondering if our day would be full of disapproving Marthas.

"Let's hope not."

Our wish was granted, but not in the way we'd hoped. There were a few more stern, conservative governess types amongst the candidates, one former school-teacher, and an American college student clearly looking for a quick visa fix. None of them quite fit the bill. They all wanted live-in situations and full-time. I could hardly blame them for that.

"Doesn't anyone just want something on the side?" I grumbled.

Smith reached down and grabbed my ankle, pulling it into his lap, he popped off my slipper and began to rub my foot. A moan spilled out of me and he chuckled under his breath.

"Never stop," I ordered him, my eyes rolling back as I relaxed into the massage.

"Not stopping is what got you into this trouble in the first place, beautiful," he reminded me in a gruff voice that sent my thoughts to darker places only he could take me.

"Shut up and rub my feet."

He obliged, his strong hands working away the stress that had plagued me the whole week. "Maybe, we need to consider hiring someone full-time."

My eyes flew open, the spell broken. "What? No." I shook my head. "I don't want someone else to raise our baby."

"I don't want that either," he said in a soothing voice. "But honestly, I don't want a stranger around her either. How do you know you can trust someone with your child if you don't know them?"

"We can have them to dinner," I said. "We don't have to live with them."

"It was just a thought." The concession was anything but. I could hear as much in his voice. He'd come back to the topic later with better ammunition for his side of the argument.

"Maybe we don't need a nanny at all."

"Beautiful," he used my nickname like a warning. "We've been over this."

"You don't want to give up Bless, and I don't want you to either. With my new office, I'm going to have my hands full."

"What's the point of moving to the country if we don't slow down? It would be easy to find a sitter in London. Jane. Edward. Clara. They'd all do it for free—and we *know* them. Plus, Buckingham comes with its own army. She'd be very safe."

I waited for him to contradict me. Instead, he continued to the next foot. He was buying time. The truth was that I'd made this point a number of times. Each time he'd managed to avoid answering me. But we both knew the reason he didn't want to be in London. He didn't want any of them watching the baby. He didn't want them around. In a way, I couldn't blame him. After everything that had happened there—to us and those we loved—staying in the city seemed like a dangerous move. But the city was full of allies not strangers. I didn't know how to make him see that.

The door opened and an unfamiliar dark head poked through the crack. "Oh, I'm so sorry. I was knocking, but..."

"Come in, Miss..."

"Ms. Welter," she said, stepping inside.

I pulled away from Smith pushing my foot back into my shoe as he stood. When I looked up, I did a double take. The woman walking into the room couldn't be more than twenty-two years-old but she was stunning. Not in your typical girl from the village way, though. She radiated confidence, managing to look posh in an ensemble I might find in my own closet down to a pair of leopard-print flats. Her dark hair, the color of bottled ink, swung around her shoulders. She smiled at me. "I didn't mean to interrupt, but Humphrey told me I could find you in here."

"It's so loud out there," I said as she bent to take a seat opposite us, smoothing her black pencil skirt down. "We should be the ones apologizing. I'm Belle. This is my husband, Smith."

"Nora," she offered, glancing around the room. "Your house is beautiful. At least, the bits that are done anyway."

"Thank you," Smith said with a laugh.

"Will it be done before the baby comes?" she asked, eying my stomach.

"I hope so," I admitted, even though I'd pretty much given up that dream. She could arrive any day and there was still the wine cellar to complete, painting to be done, and a dozen other small projects. "I'm not certain construction and infants go hand in hand."

"Babies can sleep through anything," she said with a wave of her hand, showcasing neatly trimmed and polished nails. "Of course, I'm sure you two are ready to be done with it. I imagine it's not terribly peaceful to feel as though you're on the verge of invasion all the time."

"No, it's not," Smith said. "So, why are you interested in the job?"

"It's going to sound cliché." She rolled her eyes. "But I love kids. I was studying to be a primary school teacher, but, money is tight and I thought maybe I'd take a little time off, save up, and go back part-time in the spring."

"So, you're in school?" I asked.

"Yes. Well, no. Not at the moment, I mean," she said, looking flustered for the first time since arriving. "I do want to finish, and I will. It is a part-time position, right?"

"Is that okay?" I asked, waiting for the disappointment I'd come to expect.

"Yes," she said brightly. "I'll be available a lot for those early months, when you might need me more, but I'll be able to go back in the spring, too. The timing is perfect."

Even I had to admit it was.

"Tell us more about yourself," Smith said. "Your application doesn't have a lot of history."

"I grew up in the North. I watched kids a lot when I was younger, but it seems strange to tell prospective employers to ring up your neighbor down the street. I could get some names and numbers, though, if you'd like."

"That won't be necessary," I jumped in, knowing my husband would say yes. I knew he'd run a background check on her, if he hadn't already.

"Also, I have to confess, I googled you," she said.

"Oh." I wasn't sure how to feel about that.

"And I just love the idea of Bless! It's such a good idea. I know I can't afford to buy half the outfits I fall in love with at the shops. You're a genius."

"No, not really." I shook my head, feeling put on the spot, but Smith didn't let it slide.

"She's modest. She is a genius." Smith's eyes met mine and for a moment, we were the only ones in the room. When I finally broke the spell, I discovered her watching us with a dreamy smile.

"You two are just..." She pressed a hand to her chest.

Then she shook her head a little before reaching into her bag. "Oh, I guess I should give you these. I've been certified in CPR as well as—"

A sharp knock on the door interrupted her.

"Sorry," Smith said, swiveling around. "Yes?"

The door opened to reveal Benjamin, our foreman, wearing a yellow hard hat and a grim face. "Sorry to interrupt, but we have a situation."

"A situation?" Smith repeated, already on his feet.

"You might want to come down to the wine cellar."

Smith followed him out the door, and I found myself rising, torn between going after them and propriety. I glanced at Nora, who was still holding her paperwork.

"I had no idea remodeling was so exciting," I admitted to her. "Shall we go see what new headache they've encountered?"

"I'm game." Nora dropped the papers on the table with a grin.

As soon as we stepped foot out of the reception room, I realized the house was eerily silent. All construction had stopped. That couldn't be a good sign.

"How long have you lived here?" Nora asked as we wound our way down the circular staircase to the lower ground floor where the pool, wine cellar, and storage was located.

"We're only here off and on. We still spend most of our time in the city."

"London?" she asked, sounding excited. "I'd love to live there."

"We have a house there. I guess we can't quite let go of the city life."

"I love London. Sussex has its own charms, but, honestly, I'm not sure I'd give up the city, either," she said, adding quickly, "Of course, you have a good reason."

"We'll see." I wasn't ready to commit to either Thornham or London on a permanent basis. But I couldn't help wishing whatever they'd found in the cellar would sway me one way or another.

"You should come with us, the next time we go," I found myself telling her. I liked Nora, and maybe meeting my new nanny was the excuse I needed to get Clara and Edward into the same room. Although, I'd have to come up with an Alexander-approved neutral location. If the idea of living in London excited Nora, I'm not certain she could handle being marched into Buckingham.

"Oh, I'd love that. There's a darling little children's clothing store right—"

"Ladies," Smith cut her off, slipping out of the wine cellar and blocking our path, "I think we should wrap this up upstairs."

I knew my husband well-enough to see he was ruffled. His shoulders were squared, his muscles tensed, as though he was on alert.

"What is it?" I asked in a soft voice.

Smith nudged us back toward the stairs, shaking his head. "Nothing. I'm sure it will all be fine."

Fine. There was that word again. Why did people insist on saying fine when what they meant was fucked up?

"What's going on?" I peered over his shoulder just as the cellar door swung open, giving me a glimpse of a pile of pale ivory rocks. My head turned instinctively as if it knew what I was trying to see before I'd found the right word for it: skulls.

3

SMITH

My wine cellar now sported a line of police tape, a half finished floor, and no hope of being finished by the end of the month. I'd sent Belle up for a nap hours ago in what was likely a futile attempt to keep her from getting upset. She'd handled the sight of a pile of remains found in her new home remarkably well. I wasn't sure that would hold with time.

"Mr. Price," Detective Longborn, a stump of a man with a handlebar mustache better suited to a different century, ambled toward me, scratching his head. "Someone will be by tomorrow to collect the bones. I'm sorry we can't get anyone out here sooner."

"I don't think they'll mind waiting a little longer," I said dryly.

"Looks to have been there for some time. These things happen with these old estates," he said thoughtfully. "Although there are stories about Thornham Park..."

I wasn't sure I wanted him to finish that sentence.

"Stories?"

"Superstitious nonsense they whisper about in the village. Ghosts and tragic stories," he said.

"Is that all?" I said, relieved. I didn't believe in ghosts. Not the ones that came with haunted houses, anyway. Real ghosts only exist in our memories as punishment for those we've wronged. I had those ghosts once, and Belle's love had driven them away. I wasn't scared of this house or its past after surviving that. "If there's anything we can do to speed up the investigation. My wife is due this week, and we're already cutting things close with our crews."

"Oh, I imagine there's nothing to it. We'll send them over to the London lab and I'll be in touch. Hopefully, you won't dig up any more secrets." Longborn winked at me, and I forced a grim smile.

I had plenty of secrets of mine I'd rather stay buried. I couldn't help wondering if someday, decades from now, maybe centuries, some poor bastard would dig mine up.

I waved the detectives off from the front entrance, glad to see them climbing back into their cars. It had been a long time since I'd been under the scrutiny of the authorities. It wasn't as if I was now. In fact, they'd hardly seemed phased by the discovery. I guess you get used to disturbing finds when you live somewhere with this much past.

Benjamin waited until they pulled away to deliver more bad news. "We won't be able to get back down there for a month. That crew has a new job next week and I can't pull them."

"What can we do?" I pinched the bridge of my nose, wondering if my headache was from all the racket constantly buzzing in the background or my general stress level. It wasn't that we needed the wine cellar. I wished now we hadn't even bothered to start construction on it. It had all been a pipe dream of mine to have the entire house finished before the baby made her debut. The closer we got the more anxious I felt about the situation. Maybe Belle was right and we should just stay in London rather than a half-gutted house.

I snapped my fingers. "What about this weekend?"

"We could try," Benjamin said thoughtfully, "but it would probably be an around the clock job, and I'm not certain the Mrs. will appreciate having us around all hours."

"You have a point. That's why we're going back to London," I decided, knowing I didn't need to run it by Belle. She would be thrilled, the fucking wine cellar would get done, the bones would be removed, and life might finally stand a chance of being normal for a minute or two. "I'll be reachable if there's any more problems."

"As long as we don't find a whole graveyard down there, I think I can handle it," Benjamin reassured me as I began texting the change of plans to anyone else it affected. "The men are getting ready to pack up for the night. I'll let them know we're going to be working overtime."

He said the last word with a pointed significance that didn't escape my notice. "Tell them that they'll be well-compensated if they get it done."

I'd known bribery would come into play sooner or later. I hadn't expected it to involve a body count.

Once the last of the crew cleared out, I locked the doors and headed into the kitchen. It was nearly complete, save for finishing touches. We'd removed the old marred cabinetry and put in sleek, polished cabinets, an oversized farmhouse sink, and a large island with a butcher block counter. Someday, there would be a small breakfast table in the corner where we could sit with coffee, watching our little girl eat her breakfast. Someday, life would be about simple joys. Someday would come. I just had to get through now.

There wasn't much in the fridge, given that no one had been cooking, but I managed to scrounge up some fruit and cheese as well as a bit of prosciutto that Belle had been craving lately. Piling them into my arms, I ascended the stairs to the first floor. Peeking my head into our darkened bedroom, I was greeted by a sleepy smile.

Belle lay curled on her side, a blanket half wrapped around her legs. "Did they solve the case?"

"I think it's likely going to prove to be a cold case," I said, striding over as she reached to turn on a lamp on the nightstand.

She pushed up in bed, crossing her legs under her and pulled the blanket up to her neck, shivering. "I guess a house this old has history."

"I wish the history wasn't in our wine cellar," I grumbled, opening the package of cheese for her. "We can pop into the village for a bite. I'm sure the pub's open."

"This is fine," she said, picking a grape from its stem. "I'm not that hungry."

"You're not that hungry?" I repeated, sure I'd heard her wrong.

She threw a grape at me, and it bounced off my nose. "You make me sound like a pig."

"No!" I jumped in, afraid this would spiral into a hormone-drenched misunderstanding. "You just had a swim earlier, and we never got dinner."

"I guess…" Her blue eyes darted to me before returning to study the meager spread I'd scrounged together. "It just spooked me and then with everything else, I'm too anxious to be hungry."

"Well, the spoils of our archeological digs will be removed tomorrow," I informed her, "and the wine cellar is getting done on time."

"What? How? It was already behind and now they have to wait for someone to come and take away bones." She shivered again and I realized it—and the blanket—had nothing to do with her being cold. She was genuinely frightened.

I moved closer to her, and she relaxed some. "They're going to work over the weekend to catch up on the wine cellar, and we're going to London until it's finished. The whole thing. I'm not coming back here until every last hammer has been removed from this bloody place."

She dropped the blanket, a wide smile carving across her lips. We'd made it all of it two nights in Sussex before going back to London for at least a week—if not more—and she couldn't be more pleased. "Really? I need to call Edward and Clara and—"

"Done," I stopped her. "I texted them as soon as I made the arrangements with Benjamin. I need to meet with some business associates anyway."

"Business associates?" She cocked an eyebrow. "What about friends?"

"I don't have friends," I said brusquely.

"Yes, you do."

"I have your friends who happen to usually need me to do something for them." I leaned over and kissed her forehead. "That makes us business associates."

"What about Georgia?" she pressed.

"Don't let Georgia catch you calling her a friend," I

advised. In truth, Georgia Kincaid was more than a friend to me, but not in the typical way. The bond we shared was more like those between a brother and sister. We'd both grown up under the thumb of a sinister sociopath, so like most families, our bond hinged largely on shared traumatic experiences.

"Are you going to talk to Alexander?" she asked quietly.

We'd been tiptoeing around the topic for weeks. Although we had seen our inner circle a number of times since we bought Thornham, things had shifted between all of us. Alexander, a man I butted heads with as much as I'd grown to respect him, had become increasingly insular after his wife had nearly died in a thwarted kidnapping. I couldn't blame him for being protective of her, but I hadn't been ready to swear fealty to him either. I had my own wife and child to worry about now. I knew he understood that, but it left our ends at odds with one another.

"Maybe I should invite Nora," Belle said, chewing another grape. "Get a chance to know her a little better."

"Who?" I asked, still half caught in my own thoughts.

"Nora. The last girl we interviewed," she said, screwing up her face. "I know you didn't forget her. She's gorgeous."

I tilted my head, sorting through my memories of today. There were a lot of them. "The last one? She seemed nice. I don't remember her being particularly pretty. What was her name again?"

I didn't remember. I wasn't just saying that to appease my very pregnant wife.

"No-ra," Belle said with a roll of her eyes that made me think about spanking her attitude right out of her. "And don't tell me you didn't think she was hot."

"I can't say I remember that." I shrugged. "But you liked her?"

She crossed her arms like I'd somehow offended her. "Yeah, I did—and you are seriously telling me that you didn't have the slightest attraction to her?"

"I don't think I'm the one attracted to her, beautiful." I said with a smirk. "Now I wish I remembered her better, because you're giving me all sorts of ideas about you and her."

"Oh, you'd like that, huh?" She stuck a tongue out at me. "Predictable."

"In my defense, I'm not the one who thinks she's hot."

"You're just trying to make me feel better," she said, showcasing the stubborn streak that first caught me in Belle's snares. "Because I'm fat and pregnant and she's hot and perfect and—"

"You are perfect," I cut her off, feeling the intense wave of anger I'd always felt when someone criticized my perfect wife —even when she was the one doing the damage.

"Please! Most days I wear leggings as pants," she said as though this had some meaningful contribution to reality. "I can't even see my toes anymore and sometimes when I laugh…"

"Perfect," I repeated, "and don't you dare say something negative about my wife."

"Or what?" she challenged me, her eyes lighting with a knowing gleam.

"Or *this*," I said, pulling her towards me and spinning her around so my mouth hung next to the curve of her chin. "I don't want to hear another negative word out of your mouth. You've never been more beautiful."

My hands pulled apart the sash of her silk nightgown, and it fell open, revealing the swell of her belly.

"I don't want to look at it," she mumbled, trying to pull the sash out of my hands so she could re-tie it.

"I *do*," I said, pulling her hands away and transferring them behind her back. I used the sash of her gown to tie her wrists together, taking my time even as her head lolled back onto my chest. She stared at me, her blue eyes a volatile cocktail of anticipation and mischief. She was pushing my buttons on purpose. I'd been more gentle than normal, owing to her condition. Belle, on the other hand, seemed intent on seeing how patient I could be. I would show her that I was in control. "You will not cover yourself or try to shy away from me. Do you understand?"

She nodded.

"Do. You. Understand?" I said, cupping her swollen breast in the hollow of my palm. My fingertips found the flesh of her nipple, and I readied to squeeze, already enjoying the way she squirmed.

Still she didn't answer, and I saw the corner of her lips twitch upward slightly before being tamed back to neutral. She was still trying to bait me.

It was still working.

I pinched her nipple gently, and her jaw dropped open, her face falling into a deeply relaxed, expressionless void. Her mouth formed a silent reply.

"I couldn't hear," I say, pinching harder.

There was a hiss from her sharp intake of breath.

"Yes, sir," she murmured more loudly, half moan and half taunt.

Her words turned me on like a switch. I kissed along the

curve of her chin, my hands caressing her breasts and belly, occasionally drifting toward her pussy, or as close as I could in this position, just so I could enjoy her pathetic attempts to move where she wanted me. She might have been baiting me, but now she was the one in my snare and I would decide when she came.

But this was far from being enough to release her to that welcoming dark space, she could find only at my hands—and we both knew it. I had no interest in endangering my wife while she was pregnant. No matter what she thought about the matter. Her tied hands searched the wool of my trousers until she found the bulge of my dick.

"What are you looking for, beautiful?" I teased, shifting just enough so that she could brush the rock-hard crest of my cock with her fingertips better.

"Someone needs to take charge apparently," she whined. "I suppose I have to do it."

I laughed, moving out of her reach. I had no intention of letting her have her way. She wanted an orgasm. I wanted to prove a point. Not that I wouldn't see to her needs.

"Come with me," I demanded, slipping the sash from her wrists to free them and then guiding her toward the foot of the bed.

I left her there and went to retrieve a black blindfold from the nightstand, then returned to where she stood. As I tied the silky fabric around her eyes, her hands began to reach for my dick again.

"Not yet," I admonished, moving my hips away from hers until her hands grasped at air. "I love your body. Now more than ever. Don't ever forget again."

"Yes, sir," she said demurely.

"That's better," I said, guiding her until her knees bumped gently against the edge of the bed. "Now, if you don't want to look at your perfect fucking body, I won't make you. But *I* want to look."

I circled around to the side of the bed, dropping my trousers quietly as I went and climbed in, sitting up against the headboard. "I want you to crawl to me, beautiful."

Her face beneath the blindfold morphed into a pout, but she put one knee on the end of the bed, then the other, her legs forming a triangle that pointed toward everything sacred to me: her perfect pussy and our perfect child.

She moved up the bed slowly, her long limbs languid and sure despite the changes she complained about. She sensed my legs were together, so she straddled them as she ascended, and when her hips reached mine, she practically purred with pleasure.

"You took your pants off," she said.

"I've missed fucking you. It's been a whole day," I replied, watching with a grin she couldn't see, as she rubbed her seam along my dick, bringing it to full, painful attention. "You're so gorgeous."

I reached forward and grabbed her hips, pulling them forward so my thumb could tease her clit while I worshipped her belly, planting the kind of kisses I hoped the baby wouldn't remember.

I would never have guessed how fucking turned on her pregnancy could make me. Something about the thought of her carrying my child made everything about her more intoxicating. It was the ultimate possession of her. I was rooted inside her at all times—always with her. That she only asked for more? It was almost too much.

But I would never say no. I hoped to die one day with my dick buried inside her, so that I never lived one second of not having her.

I slid my torso down from the headboard, easing her pussy over my groin until my shaft was coated with her arousal. "That's it, beautiful."

She whimpered as she lowered onto me, trembling as she took me inch by inch until her pussy had engulfed me entirely.

"Fuck, you're tight." I groaned, as I felt her clamping around my shaft, savoring the look of abandon that came over her. I moved my hips up and down slowly, watching the rise and fall of her belly, and enjoying the feel of her greedy cunt.

"I needed this," she moaned, beginning to match her timing with mine, lengthening my strokes until I could feel her clit slamming into the base of my dick, sending shudders rolling through her body.

"I love the way you look on my dick, beautiful."

"Harder, please," she said breathlessly, more a request than a demand. She knew better than to think she was on top for long.

"As you wish, beautiful."

I thrust into her as fast as I could, and each time she gasped until the moans became desperate grunts more than anything resembling words, as though the next syllable was unable to start because the last one hadn't ended. She settled into one long, endless plea. "Fuck me. Fuck me, sir!"

Still, I found myself distracted by her belly, worried that I would hurt her by being any rougher. I could care less about my orgasm as long as Belle came.

Her body went rigid, her fingers curling into fists against my chest. *"Ohhhh—"*

"That's it, beautiful," I said. "Let go."

Belle's blank expression turned to abandon, her whole body spasming against me as she rode out her climax, her fingers splaying wide to claw for better purchase as she shattered. Despite my determination not to care about my own pleasure, I couldn't help myself. The sight of my perfect, pregnant wife orgasming on my cock pushed me over the edge.

After, I laid her gently on the bed, the wispy strands of hair behind her ears damp with sweat, as I removed the blindfold.

"That was..." she began, but never finished.

I helped her into the bathroom, even offered to help her clean up—but no matter how difficult her belly might have made it, she wouldn't hear of it, excusing herself to the toilet. She emerged a minute later looking ravishing—and thoroughly ravished.

"Proud of yourself?" she teased, looking at my crooked smirk.

"A bit."

We returned to the bed, Belle seeming twice as tired as before but half as stressed.

I laid awake long after she'd fallen asleep, watching the steady rise and fall of her chest. It was an old habit, but it always calmed me. Tonight, though, my nerves remained frayed. Every time I closed my eyes, I saw that pile of bones, the skull sitting on top. I wondered if they'd slept in this house, too. I wondered if someone guarded them then. Soon, I'd find myself pacing between my sleeping wife and my sleeping daughter, watching the miracle of their breathing. I hated closing my eyes, letting her slip from my sight for even a moment felt like a betrayal of the promise I'd made myself that she'd always be safe with me. How much harder was that promise going to be to keep with sleepless nights ahead of us? Slipping from the bed, I carried the remains of our evening meal to the kitchen. Then I double checked all the locks and the security cameras. All was as it should be. Everything was in its place. Everything but the bones of strangers lying in wait in my cellar.

My feet carried me to them without thinking. I flipped on a worklamp and ducked carefully under the police tape. They'd photographed them and then laid them out in a neat orderly row. A bunch of bones that looked like femurs and ribs—but it was the skulls that stuck with me with their hairline cracks. Proof their deaths had been anything but natural. There were six of them in total, no longer piled in that gruesome pyramid I saw when I closed my eyes, but I knew exactly which one had been on top. It was the one I saw when I closed my eyes. You can't erase the sight of a skull that small from your mind.

4

BELLE

Harrods was already experiencing the holiday crush, even in October. The department store had wasted no time decorating for Christmas. A massive tree was erected outside the entrance, which meant tourists were clustered around it taking photographs. Strings of lights were hung along the building's exterior, and I was greeted with a Happy Holidays by the doorman. I resisted the urge to remind them that we were still weeks away from Christmas, knowing my ill humor regarding the matter stemmed more from being ready to give birth than any impropriety on the part of the shop. With all the preparation at the house, I hadn't even thought about getting presents. Now it occurred to me that my spontaneous shopping trip, meant to lure Edward into the open, might be the last chance I had to prepare for the upcoming holidays. I had no idea if I'd get a chance after the baby was here. Suddenly, I felt the familiar panic I'd begun to experience every time I thought about what the future held. Just as I was on the verge of hyperventilating, a man bumped his shoulder into me.

"Excuse..." the rebuke died on my lips when I turned to glare at the guilty party.

"You came!" I threw my arms around my best friend who accepted my embrace awkwardly. I pulled back to study Edward for a moment, wondering if I was overwhelming him but he simply gave me a sheepish smile.

"I don't want to squish Mini-Belle." He patted my stomach softly, looking as though he was afraid if he touched it too forcefully he might break me.

"Mini-Belle?" I repeated.

"Well, you two haven't given her a name," he explained. "Have you?"

"We have a few contenders."

"How vague of you." He spoke lightly but there was an edge coating his words, as though he didn't approve.

Of course he didn't. Edward's family was built around secrets. Secrets that had recently cost him the person he loved most in the world. It must be hard to see any kept information as innocuous after something sinister takes someone that important to you.

"I promise you will know as soon as I do."

"You could just be like us Royals and give her every name you come up with," he said dryly.

"Ah, yes, the old Louisa Anne Elizabeth Mary Victoria Fanny scenario," I said.

"Fanny?" he repeated. "Please tell me that's not a contender."

"Billie?"

"That might be worse." Despite his rough edge, the corners of his lips tipped up and he nearly smiled.

"Dare I say that you look good?" I asked, as we wove arm

and arm through the crowd in Harrods. He'd opted for a t-shirt and jeans, not his usual style, although judging by how they showed off his lean, well-toned physique I couldn't see why. Usually, he was clean-shave with his curly hair carefully coiffed into perfect submission. Today, it was hidden under a cap and he was sporting the start of either a beard or a refusal to pick up his razer. Between his hat and the sunglasses he'd kept on, he stuck out and blended in at the same time. It was hard to tell it was him under there. Although, it certainly looked like it must be someone. A few people studied us for a moment. No doubt trying to figure out who the celebrity was before giving up. He looked more like a rock star than the Prince of England.

"I look like shit," he said flatly.

"Nope." I shook my head, pausing long enough to admire a pair of Jimmy Choos. "You've got this whole devil-may-care vibe going. It's very hot."

"So is hell," he said with a shrug.

I bit my lower lip as I picked up the shoe, examining it a second longer than necessary while trying to come up with what to say. The truth was I wasn't certain how to play this. Did I ask him about David? About how he was feeling? Maybe he needed to talk. I'd tried to get him to in the beginning, but he'd been shell-shocked—and for good reason. It wasn't everyday that your husband died.

It wasn't everyday that your brother killed him.

But weeks had passed and I was worried about him. Not because he was sad. I expected that. But rather because he seemed to be retreating into himself and away from the rest of us. He'd cut off his family. He barely spoke to me. I wasn't entirely sure what he was doing with his time. Was that because I was so busy with my own domestic bliss I didn't notice? Was he avoiding me? Was I ignoring him? How did I make him feel safe to open up without pushing him too fast? Why wasn't there a how-to manual for this?

I put the shoe down with a heavy sigh.

"Too much?" Edward asked.

"When am I going to wear that in the middle of nowhere? Out to feed the chickens?"

"You have chickens?" The idea seemed to genuinely horrify him.

"And if I did?"

"You've never been much of an outdoor girl," he said, holding up his free hand in surrender and sounding genuinely amused for the first time since he arrived.

"I grew up in the countryside," I reminded him. "I can do all the important trappings of the wealthy country types: stalk deer and walk dogs and even feed chickens."

"So, is that what you're up to all the way out there?"

"Come visit and find out," I said. I'd been trying to tempt him to come with us to Sussex since this whole mess happened.

"I was thinking about going away," he said, shrugging a single shoulder like he couldn't be bothered to do more than think.

"To Sussex?" I pressed.

"Somewhere warmer." He stopped in front of a display of winter scarves and gloves. "I don't think I want to deal with winter in England this year."

"But you'll be here for Christmas?" I asked in a soft voice.

"I don't know. I find I don't really feel like celebrating this year." He fingered the rough edge of a Burberry scarf. "It would be our anniversary, you know."

"I know. I don't think you should be alone."

Edward licked his lower lip, and I found myself wishing I could see his eyes. The last thing he needed was to be alone on his first anniversary. But was spending it with me, my husband and our daughter going to be better? Or just a painful reminder of what he'd lost?

"I thought I'd find a beach somewhere with cold drinks and hot men. Who says I have to be alone for Christmas? I'm not the only single gay man in the world." His lips quirked into a lopsided grin that was too forced to be believable.

As long as the wound was open, I might as well pour all the salt in with one go. "Clara wants to have lunch."

"Tell her I said hello," he murmured.

"She wants you to come."

"I'm not going there. Wherever she is...he is."

I didn't have to ask what he meant. Alexander and Clara had a tendency to orbit one another since they met. That had only gotten worse given everything they went through. "I'm sure we can arrange it, so that he stays away. Don't you want to see Wills?"

"Does it make me a bad person if I say no?" he asked in a hollow voice. "I don't want to hate her, but I can't seem to..."

Forgive her. "She didn't do anything wrong."

"I know." He nodded his head before allowing it to hang forward. "But trying to reason with the heart is about as effective as arguing with a table. It can't be done. I just need time."

"Then that's what I'll tell her," I said simply. It hurt to see him go through this. It hurt to watch Clara blame herself. But sometimes the only thing that healed wounds was time.

"Belle," he said tentatively, lowering his sunglasses to stare at me from red-rimmed eyes, "don't tell her that I hate her. I don't really..."

"I won't," I promised him, wrapping him in another hug only to feel the baby kick hard.

Edward pulled back, his glasses still pushed low on his nose and his eyes wide. "Was that?"

"Yep," I said with a laugh. "She's growing quite demanding."

"I warned you about squishing Mini-Belle," he said with a laugh that lifted some of the weight from the air around us. "If you aren't careful, she'll be forced to come out here and tell you off."

"Promise?" I groaned. My due date was only two days away and there was no end in sight.

"If she's anything like her mother, she'll show up when she damn well pleases," Edward teased. We rounded a corner and nearly ran into a Christmas tree trimmed with artisan, blown glass ornaments. His good mood evaporated. Maybe shopping wasn't such a good idea, after all. I could get presents later or place an order. Right now, he needed me more than anyone else in my life might need a gift weeks from now.

"Are you hungry?" I blurted out, steering him clear of the reminder of the impending holidays.

"I could eat, but only if it's something full of carbs that will make me emotionally numb," he demanded.

"I think we can make that happen." It wasn't much. Maybe it was all I could do: try to be there when he needed to fall apart. Maybe that's all anyone can do when dealing with a broken heart.

5

SMITH

The bar of the Westminster Royal was fairly quiet given the time of day. A few businessmen lingered over cocktails, discussing market prices and valuations. A couple, obviously mind-affair, were sipping champagne in the corner. I took a table in the middle of the room, where I'd be able to see every entrance and exit and waited for my guest to arrive. Out of habit, I checked my mobile, concerned that if Belle tried to reach me I might not have heard it in the bustle of London's sidewalks. No new messages. I expected a call any moment —*the* call— and the longer I went without receiving it the more tightly wound I became. It was difficult to let Belle out of my sight when she might go into labor at any time.

Across from me a table of businessmen stopped talking and turned to stare at a woman entering the bar. I didn't have to look to see who it was.

Georgia Kincaid always made an entrance, whether she was trying to or not.

Today she'd traded her usual motorcycle leather for a pair of tight black pants and a fitted blazer that dipped low enough to display the lace of her bra. Her glossy black hair swung loosely around her shoulders, contrasting sharply with her ruby red lips. She didn't bother to smile when she spotted me. Instead, she strode straight toward me, ignoring the men's stares, and took the seat next to me, the only other chair that afforded views of the exits. Some habits never died, and Georgia's current line of work necessitated vigilance.

"Where's your wife?" Georgia asked, peering around me like I might be hiding a nine-months pregnant Belle behind my back.

"Shopping with Edward," I said in a clipped tone.

"I don't think you have to worry about him." Georgia's lips twitched into a bemused smile.

"He's not the one I'm worried about."

"You can't keep her under lock and key all the time," she advised with a sigh.

I shot her a look. "Can't I? Isn't that what your boss does?"

It was something of a sore subject that Georgia had gone to work for Alexander. Particularly, because I'd planned to coax her into keeping an eye on Belle. Somehow, she'd been talked into working for the monarchy, which, given how we were raised, had more than surprised me. Georgia and I had spent our formative years being groomed by one of England's most insidious crime lords to hate the Royal family and everything it stood for. I'd thought for years that no one hated them more than me, Georgia, and my surrogate father, Hammond. I'd been expected to work against them by Hammond until I realized I wanted nothing to do with him or his sins. I'd had to lose the thing I thought was most important to me in the world: my wife. Then, I'd had to discover my marriage had been a manipulation. That's when I convinced Georgia to start working against Hammond with the help of the Royal family. But the deeper we dove, the uglier it got until Hammond delivered a game-changer to my door: Belle. I wasn't supposed to fall in love with her. Alexander had been furious, concerned it would jeopardize his investigation into the assassination of his father. That's when I realized my loyalty would only ever lie with Belle. But even that hadn't been simple. It turned out that we were nothing but pawns in a much larger game. I'd won my freedom only to be dragged back into the fray when they kidnapped Belle's best friend. I'd helped Alexander find his wife for Belle's sake. Each time I got pulled back into that world, I wondered if I'd make it back out. This last time, my alliance with Alexander had felt dangerously like friendship.

It's why I had to convince Belle to leave London. She was in danger as long as we remained near them. But keeping her from her closest friends was proving to be more than I could handle. It wasn't that I wanted to isolate her. More than anything I wanted her to make new friends, settle into life in Sussex, and start over. Georgia could have helped with that, but I suspected that she'd actually fallen victim to caring about Alexander and Clara too much to walk away.

"Don't drag Alexander into this," Georgia advised. "This isn't about him."

"Everything's about him," I said gruffly. That's how it felt in London.

"He's the King, so it probably feels that way."

"He convinced you to take a job working for the good guys," I said, wondering how someone as chaotic as Georgia had found herself actively working for the Crown.

"The benefits are excellent," she said with a shrug. "You should see my new ride."

I raised an eyebrow. I'd much rather chat about cars than royalty.

"Porsche Panamera," she said. "Black, naturally."

"That seems a little fast and loose for Buckingham." I had to admit I was impressed. The Porsche wasn't just another armored vehicle. It had some style to it, as well as three millimeters of ballistic steel on its roof and floor board in addition to its bulletproof exterior. It was a good choice for someone who drove around the Queen, but not the safest on the market.

"He tried to get me in a Mulsanne, but I told him I wasn't on my way to the Care Home yet, so he had to budge."

"The Mulsanne is safer," I said with a shrug. "It would have been my choice."

Georgia whipped around to stare at me, her dark eyes, rimmed in coal-black liner, narrowed like she was dissecting me.

"What?" I shrugged.

"I'm trying to decide if you've been replaced by an imposter. The Smith Price I know would never choose that Bentley over a Porsche," she said.

"I have different priorities now."

"I guess we all have to grow up someday." But she sounded less than enthused about my sudden maturity. "Did Belle take your balls as well as the keys to the Bugatti?"

"She wouldn't let me sell the Bugatti. She's rather attached to it." I'd been willing to part with my former daily car, which would have nearly paid for our new home entirely, but my wife wouldn't hear of it. Given the memories we'd made in it, I couldn't exactly blame her. But that didn't mean we'd be bringing our baby home in its boot. "We got a Range Rover. It made sense."

"If you're going to keep being so bloody rational, I'm going to need a drink, or at least a good whipping," she said, but there was an edge of laughter in her voice.

Could it be that Georgia Kincaid found this funny? Maybe even charming?

She really had softened up during her time with Clara.

I raised my hand to call over the waiter, who appeared with the promptness of a man who recognized when alcohol was necessary. I ordered two Macallans and he disappeared to the bar.

"So, what brings you to London?" Georgia asked, leaning back in her seat.

"I can't visit?"

"I thought your entire plan was to get your wife as far away from this mess as possible before she shot out your progeny. Isn't she due any minute?"

"The doctor said it's likely she'll go past dates since it's our first." Until my wife had gotten pregnant, I thought I knew everything there was to know about her body, having made an extensive study of it. The past few months had proven me wrong.

"And you were dying to catch up with me?" Georgia enjoyed baiting the hook. If the situation called for it, she could be direct to the point of painfulness. But if you came to her, clearly wanting something, she was going to make you work for it. It was her way.

"I need a favor." There was no point in continuing with the pleasantries. We were both busy people, and while she might be considered my oldest friend, we'd never exactly confided in one another.

"A favor? I'm shocked." She smiled up at the waiter as he dropped off the Scotch, and the poor man nearly tripped over his own feet. I could never tell if the way men reacted to her was out of lust or survival instinct—or some primitive combination of the two.

"They found something at my house."

"Sounds ominous," she admitted.

"Bones."

Her glass paused mid-way to her mouth, an eyebrow arching. "Bones?"

"Of the human variety," I answered her unspoken question. "The local police don't think anything of it."

"Isn't it like a million years-old? There's bound to be a few bodies in the basement." Her slender shoulder lifted and I was reminded of a time when I could have been so nonchalant about a discovery of this nature.

"I would have said the same thing, but the Detective said something that made me wonder if they left something out of the real estate listing." I recounted my conversation with Longborn to her.

"It sounds like country superstitions, Smith," she said when I finished.

She had a point. I'd been telling myself the same thing all day. "It probably is, but I suppose I'd rather know what I'm dealing with than listen to rumors."

"Are you asking me to find out if your house is haunted?" There was the bluntness I knew her for.

"I'm asking you to find out about its history," I clarified. "I don't believe in ghosts."

"If you don't believe in ghosts, then just see it for what it is: a pile of bones in an old house." She sipped her drink, her eyes shutting as realization dawned on her. "It scared her, didn't it?"

"A little." It felt like a betrayal to reveal that Belle had been upset by the discovery. She wouldn't want Georgia to see any weakness in her. "She's uncertain about the move. I'd rather not have any more surprises. If we know exactly what we're dealing with, we can avoid that."

"I'll look into it." Georgia placed her glass on the table and folded her hands, taking a deep breath. "There's something else I should tell you."

I braced myself for whatever bomb she was going to drop. With Georgia, I never knew what to expect, only that there would be fallout.

"I'm not sure you're going to be happy about this…"

"What?" I growled.

"Just, remember not to shoot the messenger. It's about your place in Holland Park."

"What about it?" I asked slowly. Belle had met up with Edward as soon as we arrived, and I'd been focused on tying up loose ends in the city. We hadn't been to our townhouse yet, but given that Thornham would be uninhabitable for days if not weeks, we'd planned to meet there this evening.

"You should see for yourself," Georgia warned me, "and, Price, you probably want your wife to see it, too."

BELLE

It's never reassuring to get a phone call from your husband telling you he'll be picking you up in five minutes. I had no idea how Smith knew I was at CoCo's with Edward. I told myself he'd simply remembered that I used to frequent the Notting Hill restaurant with my friends back in the day. But Smith and I had barely known each other then, and try as I might to dismiss his brusque demand, I suspected he was tracking my phone. After what had happened to Clara, I understood his paranoia. Truth be told, I almost appreciated it. But we weren't high-value public figures. People didn't know who we were and our enemies were dead. At times, I had to remind myself that old habits die hard. The longer we continued living in peace, the more it would soothe my husband. I just had to put up with a little over-protectiveness until then.

"Come with us," I urged Edward as we stepped onto the sidewalk outside. I flipped the collar of my coat up against the light drizzle that had started while we were inside gorging on fettuccine.

Edward paused, as though he was honestly considering it, before shaking his head. "I'm not sure being around a happily married couple is the best idea for me right now. No matter how much I love you."

I didn't miss the singular aspect of his proclamation. Edward got along with Smith, but they weren't exactly close. Really no one was close to my husband. He had something of the beast in him, which put off most people. Not that Smith minded. In fact, he seemed to prefer it that way. I still couldn't understand how I'd managed to get past the armour he kept so carefully in place. I only wished he'd let someone else in, too. As much as I loved my husband, I was grateful to have friends I could rely on.

"But you'll visit when the baby comes, right?" There was no way I was letting him worm his way out of that one.

"I don't know. I was thinking about taking a trip. I might not be back in time," he said with the air of someone who'd just been asked out on an awkward date.

"Another one?" I snapped, momentarily losing my patience with him. He was going to skip Christmas. Wasn't that enough? I took a deep breath and shook off my frustration. "I don't want you to miss this."

He gave me a tight smile. "Says the woman who eloped in New York."

"That was different."

To his credit, he didn't point out that I was being a hypocrite. He simply raised one eyebrow. "Look, it has nothing to do with you. I just need to get away from this city. Everywhere I look, I see him. But it's more than that. I don't see him how he was. I don't trust any of those memories. He was lying to me the whole time. Nothing we had was real. I can't even miss him properly."

I placed a hand on his arm, feeling like a bitch for losing my temper and letting my hormones get the better of me. "You have every right to your grief. David did love you. I'm certain of that."

"Then why did he do it? I thought I knew him better than anyone in the world," he admitted in a low voice as a group of laughing friends jostled past us into the restaurant. "He had a whole life he kept from me."

I thought of Smith and how complicated our relationship was in the beginning. He'd guarded himself and his secrets. It had taken a long time to develop trust between us, but even now I knew there were places deep inside him locked away from me. I suspected they were locked away from him, too. "There's always unknown places in another person, no matter how much you love them or they love you."

"That's supposed to be what marriage is about," Edward exploded, startling two women walking past with shopping bags. They huddled closer together and quickly crossed the street. "You find those places—discover them. *Together*. The good ones and the bad ones. You spend the rest of your life committed to exploring that person until you can read them like a well-worn map."

Maybe he was right. Isn't that what I wanted? To know Smith like I knew myself. Isn't that what I wanted him to do as well? Discover me? Explore me? Until there was no unknown territory between us. It was the kind of work that took time and commitment.

"We didn't get that," he continued, this time more calmly. "And the worst part is that sometimes, I wonder..."

I waited for him to tell me, sensing a confession forming. He opened his mouth as a honk startled me from behind.

I turned to see our new Range Rover pulled to the curb, its headlights illuminating the misty rain. Smith jumped out of the car, frowning, to find me outside. I moved between him and Edward instinctively, knowing that my husband shouldn't choose this moment to chew him out for letting me stand in the rain.

"Just a moment," I ordered him, earning a sharp look of disapproval. But Smith held his tongue. Pivoting back to Edward, I wrapped him in a warm hug, lowering my voice so only he could hear me. "I am always here for you. No judgments. No expectations."

"Let me know when you deliver that little hen," he whispered back. "I promise to come as soon as I can."

"I know you will."

It was the most I could ask of him. I wanted my best friend to be there, but I also wanted him to heal. Maybe I could help him with that. Maybe some pain had to be faced alone.

An umbrella swung over my head, and I glanced up to see Smith standing there with a stony face, a sweep of dark hair falling across his eyes. His black coat was buttoned high at his neck, hugging his formidable upper body and he wore black leather gloves with notched holes at the knuckles. In the clouds and hazy twilight, he looked like a dark angel. Not the kind that came to deliver good news, but the ones who visited fury and vengeance upon the earth. I shivered.

Would I ever know all of him? Did I want to?

"Beautiful," he said gently but firmly.

I pecked Edward's cheek, squeezing his hand goodbye.

Smith walked me back to the car, holding the umbrella over my head, his other hand pressed protectively against the small of my back. When I climbed inside, he paused to make certain my seat belt was correctly positioned under the place where our baby girl grew before brushing his lips over mine. Even the small act left me breathless. It reminded me that while I might not ever reach every dark place inside him, it was all open to me. He'd unlocked all the doors. I chose which ones to step through. Settling back in my seat as he circled round to the driver's side, I decided that was more than most people could ever ask for.

"Is it warm enough?" he asked as he shifted into drive and pulled out behind a taxi cab.

"Toasty," I promised. I hadn't realized I was cold until I got inside the warm and dry interior cabin. I wiggled my toes, helping them thaw faster.

"Why were you in the rain?"

I rolled my eyes. "Because my bear of a husband told me to be ready to go in five minutes, and it took him ten to arrive."

That shut him up.

"Where are we going?" I asked. He hadn't bothered with specifics when he called. In fact, he'd sounded rather uneasy when we spoke.

"The house." He hesitated, stealing a glance at me.

"Our house? What's wrong?" I frowned.

"I met with Georgia this afternoon. She told me that..."

"What?"

"I don't actually know." The car slowed as we turned onto Holland Park into a traffic jam. He tapped the leather-bound steering wheel impatiently. "What is going on here?"

"We were only in Sussex for two days. Don't tell me that you already forgot the traffic." I said dryly, but he didn't laugh.

He craned his head, trying to see around the back-up of vehicles in front of us. He really was worried, which only made me feel more panicked.

"What exactly did she say?" I asked.

"That we needed to go by the house. That we should see it in person." A car next to us turned and Smith guided us over, moving us incrementally closer to whatever disaster awaited us in Holland Park.

This couldn't be happening. I wasn't ready to commit to Thornham. I thought I had more time, but if something had gone wrong at our home in the city, what choice did I have? Convincing Smith that we needed a new London residence was unlikely. Never mind that we would have nowhere to stay tonight. I could call Clara and we could go there, but I doubted Smith would be fond of that idea. I was supposed to have more time. I rubbed circles on my belly. She would be here any day, but I wasn't ready to fully give up my life in London. Not until she came or we felt ready to be on our own.

Or maybe ever.

The more time I spent in London, the more I wondered if I could give it up to move back to the country. What was I supposed to do with my time there? Make menus for the cook to prepare and wander the grounds? Adopt a few dogs? Take up hunting? What had I been thinking?

I opened my mouth to spill all of my thoughts to Smith when the traffic opened up and we plunged past the lane next to us, turning onto the street that led us home.

From the outside nothing looked wrong. It was the same

stately townhome, the same cozy street, the same quiet, sleepy vibe, I'd expected to find. The windows were dark, though, and that was odd. After making the mutual decision not to hire staff in London, given they had a disturbing tendency to be spying on us in the past, Smith had installed an electronic surveillance system that allowed us to keep an eye on the house, turn lights off and on, even unlock doors remotely in case we needed to let someone in. Georgia was on the list of people who had access, given that she was much closer in case of emergency.

"I thought we had the lights set to go on in the evening?" I asked. It was a precaution meant to make the house look occupied to potential thieves.

"We do," he said grimly. He maneuvered the car to an empty spot on the street in front of the house and parked. "Stay here."

"Like hell," I said. "Georgia said we should both see it."

"If there's someone in there," he growled.

I shook my head, unimpressed by the alpha male on display and opened my door. "She would have told us that! I bet the stupid system isn't working. You know she didn't approve of it."

"I trust a computer more than a man," he said.

"There's a man behind the computer," I pointed out as he joined me outside the car. I held out my hand, and he took it, somewhat grudgingly. We climbed the steps to the house, Smith fumbling with the app on his phone. But when we reached the door, it was already cracked open.

"For fuck's sake," Smith bit out, his forehead furrowing.

"You didn't do that?" I tried not to let my sudden nervousness slip through.

"No. You're right. Georgia wanted to show us the bloody thing is broken. I'll call out the company tomorrow."

"But tonight?" I felt uneasy staying here now. What if the doors unlocked overnight and we woke to find someone in our house? Smith would protect us at any cost. I'd learned that lesson before. I didn't want my husband to have more blood on his hands, though.

"Wait here," Smith ordered. This time I didn't argue as he opened the door and reached for the light switch as the overhead chandelier burst on followed by a loud chorus of "surprise."

Thank God my husband didn't carry a gun anymore. And if looks could kill, the one he was shooting our family and friends might have taken the lot. I released the breath I'd been holding and laughed, shaking his arm, as Georgia stepped from behind the group with a sly smile on her face.

"Sorry, Price. They made me do it," she said.

He glared at her. "Remind me to take you off as a point of contact."

Smith might not be pleased, but my heart swelled seeing all the people I loved in one place. My Aunt Jane was here, speaking to my brother John. It was a bit surprising to see him here, but I was glad what little family I had made the occasion. I spotted my mother, pouting in the back of the crowd. She had yet to accept that she was going to be a grandmother or that I'd given the family estate to her step-son. She saw both moves as betrayals. But it was the shining smile at the front of the small cluster that sent tears to my eyes.

Clara Bishop, my best friend, had been through hell this year, and here she was front and center, smiling to celebrate my new baby. The children were absent and she was holding a glass of champagne. I was instantly jealous. She looked gorgeous, flushed and happy, her curves on display in a fitted cashmere sweater the color of fresh cream and thick, black ponté leggings. Her silky brunette hair looked like she'd just stepped out of the salon and her make-up was minimal but perfectly applied. I bit back a grin thinking about the girl I'd known at university. Then, she'd worn jeans and t-shirts with no interest in fashion much to my dismay. When she'd met the Prince of England, she'd embarked on a style makeover worthy of a reality show. Now, she looked every bit the queen she was.

"Are you to blame for this?" I asked as she sauntered forward.

"I couldn't let my best friend have a baby without giving her one last hurrah." She threw her free arm around me and I used the momentary distraction to swipe her champagne flute.

I took a delicate sip and groaned before passing it back to her.

"I'll bring you some in the hospital," she promised with a sympathetic grin. "Unless, you're going to have the baby..."

"No, we both agreed to have her here," I said. At least, Smith and I had agreed on that. "I think he's going to kick everyone else out of the Lindo Wing."

Clara laughed, but I spotted a dark shadow flicker over her face before vanishing. She hadn't spoken much about the birth of her son, William, but I knew parts of the day haunted her. They probably always would.

"Where's Alexander?" I asked, looking around for her husband.

"Home with the children. He won't let anyone watch

them but you and Georgia and Norris," she admitted with a whisper, "and Norris and Georgia couldn't change a nappy if their lives depended on it. One of them is going to have to learn or I'll be forced to give my mother the keys to Buckingham."

"You have me," I said, feigning offense.

"I think your days are numbered," she said, looking me over. "And I thought I'd finally lost you to the country."

"We're back for a while."

"You just left two days ago!" But she looked nothing but pleased by this revelation. "Elizabeth misses you. She threw a tantrum when Alexander told her where I was going."

"I'll come by tomorrow." Life felt right back in London. Here I could make spontaneous plans to visit my godchildren, grab a bite with my best friend, and go home to a quiet house with my husband. "Is Edward here?"

I suddenly realized why he'd hesitated when I asked him to come along. He'd known about the baby shower and managed to keep it a secret.

Clara flinched, shaking her head slightly. "I thought he would come...especially, when I messaged him that Alexander wouldn't be here. I guess he's avoiding all of us."

I didn't have the heart to tell her that I'd seen him this afternoon. They would work this out with time, but I heard the pain in her voice. She loved him like he was her own brother. Him choosing not to come told her the thing she feared the most: he wasn't just avoiding Alexander, he didn't want to see her either.

"He was probably busy. I mean, I don't see your sister here either," I pointed out, trying to distract her as we walked arm and arm into the living room where dozens of delicate pink roses had been used to decorate the mantle and window sills. The table in the corner was laid out with platters of sweets, including a five-tiered stand showcasing mini petit-fours each featuring a sugar tiara. Clara picked up a champagne flute filled with orange juice and passed it to me.

"Parties are less fun when you're pregnant," I grumbled.

"You can have as much cake as you want, though." She pulled me toward the corner, lowering her voice conspiratorially. "Lola is in Silverstone."

"Again?"

Clara's sister, Lola, was also my business partner. Given that our company, Bless, was almost entirely online and now boasted five employees to handle the work of shipping and stocking, she and I were free to work wherever we wanted—and lately, Lola had been doing double time working with Anderson Stone, who, apart from being a world-famous race car driver, was also Alexander's half-brother. Lola had been dispatched to help acclimate to the sudden frenzy of interest from the media when the truth was revealed. Neither Alexander nor Anders had known about one another, there was a lot to tackle, and Lola had taken charge of it.

"If I didn't know better..." Clara let her thought trail off, her eyes flashing wickedly.

"But she hates him," I said with a laugh, knowing exactly what she was thinking. "She told me so herself."

"It's a relief to have her there," Clara confided. "With everything else going on. But we are not talking about that tonight, because there are sweets and presents and this mama has the night off!"

"I can't believe Alexander let you out of his sight," I admitted.

"He sent Norris." She tilted her head to Alexander's long-time friend, bodyguard, and advisor who was busy chatting with my Aunt Jane. Jane was making no attempt to hide her flirtations, even from here.

"That would be an interesting match," I murmured.

"I just want everyone to have their own happy endings," Clara said thoughtfully before taking a deep breath. We both knew that happiness didn't mean perfection when it came to love. It just meant someone who made all the hard bits worth it.

"Are we going to open presents?" My mother appeared next to us, looking directly at Clara like I wasn't there. "I have an appointment in the morning."

I forced myself to lean over and kiss her cheek. My mother wasn't an easy woman to love. In all honesty, I wasn't certain that I did love her, but the importance of familial duty had been drilled into me at a young age.

"Belle," she said in a snide tone, accepting the kiss without returning it, "you look tired. Have you seen your doctor?"

"Tomorrow," I told her. "I'm hoping that she'll evict this little one."

"Well, you really don't want to go much longer." She eyed me carefully and I could see her counting up my flaws like she was tallying a register. "How much weight have you put on?"

"Mary," Smith's stern voice broke through before the full weight of her words could strike, "lovely to see you."

My mother smiled in a way that was more grimace than greeting and excused herself.

"Sometimes when I think my mother is bad, I remember your mother and I'm thankful," Clara said thoughtfully. She wrapped an arm around me. "You haven't gained an ounce. You just look like you swallowed a bowling ball."

I knew she was lying, but it was well-meant. There was a time when my mother's remarks would have hurt, but I was past that now. I'd gained some weight and a lot of curves—which was not only normal, but healthy—and it wasn't like my husband was complaining.

"I stopped caring about what she thought a long time ago," I said, waving off their concern, "but she brought up a good point. Presents?"

"As you wish." Clara clapped and called out for everyone to gather round.

It turned out that a chair had been specifically designated for my use: new upholstered rocking chair, a gift from my Aunt Jane. I spent the next hour unwrapping tiny baby things. Booties and bonnets and tiny, knee socks. It was almost impossible to believe she would be here soon and that these would fit her. They looked like they were meant for a doll. By the time I was finished, I was surrounded by a mountain of wrapping paper and half the nursery selection of Harrods.

"This is going to be a well-dressed baby," Jane said from her seat near the hearth.

"There's one more," Clara said, passing a small box to me with a smile.

I looked at the pretty package, checking for a card or even just a tag. "Okay, out with it, who brought it?"

No one spoke up. My eyes flickered to Smith, wondering if he'd managed to sneak in a gift without me noticing, but he looked as puzzled as I felt. I untied the pink bow and opened the lid of the box. Inside, I found a small, velvet jewelry box. I couldn't bite back a smile. Of course, Smith had something ready, even without knowing there was going to be a party. I shot him a bemused glance, but he continued to feign innocence. When I lifted the velvet box, he took a step closer, his expression giving way to concern. My fingers paused on the lid as I realized he really didn't know where it had come from.

"Maybe you shouldn't..." he began as I popped open the lid. Nestled inside was one single copper bullet.

7

SMITH

Georgia lingered after the other guests had gone. The evening's final present had considerably dimmed the mood. Poor Clara looked on the edge of a nervous collapse when Norris took her home to Alexander. I had a feeling he wouldn't be allowing her out again anytime soon. The trouble was that it wasn't just any copper bullet. It was the copper bullet. The one I'd saved for Hammond but never used. The trouble is that I knew exactly where that bullet was supposed to be, and it wasn't in a velvet box in Holland Park. Tonight, Clara would go home and tell Alexander the story. I would be paying him a visit soon, so he could explain how a bullet from a gun I gave him for safekeeping made its way to my wife's baby shower.

He wouldn't have an answer for me. It didn't matter. The message was clear enough: I was right. London wasn't safe for us anymore. We'd gambled by staying linked to the royals. Now there was a price to pay.

"Tell Alexander I want to see him as soon as possible," I told Georgia.

Her eyebrow arched. "That sounds like an order. He won't like that."

"But you'll love delivering that message," I said flatly.

"What is this about?" she asked. "That looked like the bullet you'd saved for Hammond."

"It was." I checked the lock of the back door as she followed alongside me. Then I began checking every window. "How long was the door unlocked tonight?"

"I let them in myself. No one was in the house without me present." She sounded almost apologetic. "If I had known..."

I ignored her guilt. If Georgia had been here when the package was delivered, she would have seen who'd brought it. That meant it had slipped in with one of the evening's guests. The problem was that we trusted all of them implicitly. I pulled up the security system's app on my phone and began looking through recordings. It provided a list of every time a door or window opened. I watched each silently, Georgia hovering nearby, until I reached our own arrival. "You have a bigger problem than a single bullet. Whoever delivered it didn't bring it to the house themselves. One of the guests did."

"There was no one here that would have done that."

My eyes closed as I felt a headache coming on. "Exactly."

"I'll call someone to watch the house tonight, so you can get some sleep. I'm sure we can arrange a security detail while you're in town. I'll speak with—"

"No," I cut her off. "I don't trust Alexander's men."

"They're my men," she said coldly.

"And you know all of them? You *trust* all of them?"

"I don't trust anyone," she reminded me. "Except..."

"Who?" That was who I wanted here until I could figure out how to handle this situation on my own. I'd be retrieving my father's gun from Alexander—if it hadn't been taken as well.

"Brexton," she said, "but he's doing double time keeping an eye on Anders."

"Get him here." If MI-18, the shadowy society that had dark plans for the royal family, had any interest in Anders, they could have taken him out a long time ago. The threat to Belle was immediate. I could sense it. "Wait, Brex knew about the bullet."

I'd shown it to him as proof that I wasn't the one who killed Hammond when he came knocking on my door two Christmases ago. I had no reason not to trust Brexton Miles, but I couldn't claim to know him well enough not to mention it.

Georgia shook her head. "There's no way. Brex is an open book."

It sounded like there was a story there, but she wasn't going to share it with me. "Then, I want him. You can tell Alexander he's coming back to London."

"He's not going to like that."

"He owes me," I said in a clipped tone. "I'll remind him of that when we meet."

Georgia didn't try to reason with me further. She knew better. "You should get some rest. Once the baby gets here, you won't be sleeping much."

Despite everything that happened tonight, I couldn't help smiling. The baby was the light in all this darkness. Soon, we'd meet the proof of our love. We'd be a family, and I would do anything to protect my child and her mother. "I won't mind being tired then."

Georgia started toward the front door and I walked

behind her. She drew her coat off a hanger by the door. "Is there anyone else who knew about that bullet? The one you'd saved for Hammond?"

"No one alive." I'd already asked myself that question. I couldn't blame her for wondering.

"Maybe this doesn't have anything to do with MI-18."

"Do you really believe that?" All our troubles led back to them. It had taken years for us to put a name to the faceless organization. "No one else alive knows about that bullet, except you, Belle, and Alexander. Do you think one of them did it?"

"They want him," she said softly. "Not to bruise your ego, Price, but why would they be interested in you now? You're out."

"I helped him. I stuck my neck out." And now it was back on the chopping block.

She studied me for a moment, her dark eyes veiled in secrets before she turned toward the door. Georgia was down the first step before curiosity got the better of me.

"What are you thinking?" I called behind her.

She stopped, not bothering to turn to address me, but I heard her voice cut through the crisp night. "I guess people really do change."

CHANGE? I TURNED THE WORD OVER IN MY HEAD AS I locked the front door, taking special care to throw the additional manual bolts not connected to the security system. The surveillance feed might not have shown anyone entering the premises but it also had not alerted me that my system was down earlier. That had been a harmless manipulation on

Georgia's part for the baby shower, but it was a good reminder that even a computer system could be deceived. While we were in Sussex, I didn't care if someone broke in here, trashed the place, stole my shit. But while my most priceless possession slept upstairs, I wanted to know she was safe.

I climbed the stairs, remembering a simple time when I would have spent tonight fucking Belle on them before watching her crawl to the bedroom, dripping with me. Now everything was changing. I was on the verge of having everything I wanted: her, a family, a future. Suddenly Thornham and its silly ghost stories looked even more appealing. The real ghosts were in London. This was where I'd committed my sins. This was where my bodies were buried.

I paused in the hall, realizing how empty the house felt now. We'd never bothered to do much to it. Never hung art on the second floor. Anytime, we'd gotten close to a bed, we wound up in it, thwarting thoughts of decorating. It hadn't been the same in Sussex. We'd relaxed there. We'd planned. We'd picked out bloody curtain rods for an entire day, and I'd never been so happy.

Inside our bedroom, I found Belle slipping on a silk kimono. It closed under her bust, fluttering open over her belly. My breath caught for a moment as I looked at her. She looked up, grinning sheepishly. "It doesn't fit."

She'd managed to maintain a good attitude about the evening's events, but I worried that she might be on the verge of a breakdown. Between Thornham's skeletons and cryptic, but sinister gift deliveries, it was too much. She should be focusing on the birth of our daughter, soaking up the last few days of being a couple before we became a family of three.

"You look pensive," she said unhappily.

I shook my head, determined to leave our troubles outside the bedroom. We should have one safe place.

"Fine." She sighed, sweeping her hair into a knot on top of her head. "I'll say it. Someone sent me Hammond's bullet. I didn't want to talk about it in front of everyone, but we should talk about it."

"There's nothing to talk about. Georgia is looking into it." I decided to leave out that we'd have a security detail soon. She'd find out soon enough.

"Nothing to talk about?" She turned, arms crossed, her lips still sporting her signature crimson shade although the rest of her make-up had been removed. "It's not your job to carry all the burdens of the past."

"It is—" I held a hand to stop her from interrupting me "—while you're pregnant. You're carrying the most important part of our family right now. Let me handle this."

Her open mouth closed. I waited, but she seemed struck silent by my request.

"Beautiful." I crossed to her and took her in my arms. "Nothing can tear us apart, remember? You and me? We're forever."

"I just want a break from it," she admitted, nuzzling against my chin. "From the construction and the drama and the swelling ankles."

"I can do something about that." I led her to the bed, and she licked her lips in anticipation as I dropped to my knees before her. Picking up one foot, I rubbed her ankle.

She groaned. "Should I be concerned that foot rubs are becoming our go-to foreplay?"

"This isn't foreplay." I said, shushing her. "I'm just taking care of my wife."

"So you don't want sex?" she teased.

My eyes traveled to where her knees were parted slightly. "I've heard it can induce labor."

"Orgasms can," she corrected me.

"In that case." I abandoned her foot. I stood and offered her my hand. She was breathtaking as I helped her to her feet. Certain, but tentative. Wicked, but innocent. Nothing I ever expected, everything I ever wanted.

I led her to the tall armoire in the corner and opened its door. She waited with curious eyes as I slipped off my jacket and reached for a hanger.

"You're going to make me beg, aren't you?" she murmured with a knowing smile, but I shook my head.

"No, beautiful. Although, I love when you beg." I pressed my thumb to her lower lip, pushing it down and smearing her red lipstick ever so slightly. Belle gasped with pleasure, flicking her tongue over its tip. "Give me your hands."

She held them out, crossing them at the wrists as I'd trained her. I smirked as I slipped the sash from her robe, marveling at my perfect plaything. Then I slid the kimono from her shoulders, allowing it to flutter like falling petals to rest at her feet.

"You're going to stay very still," I informed her, reaching for an empty hanger, "and let me give you the orgasms. You're to come hard as many times as I choose, but you don't have to ask for permission. Understood?"

"Yes, Sir," she breathed.

I tied the sash around her wrists, leaving a small loop but knotting it tightly.

"Over your head," I ordered.

She lifted her arms obligingly, and I backed her against

the door of the armoire, allowing it to close to a mere crack behind her. I reached up with the hanger, slipping the loop of the sash over its hook before hanging it over the top of the door. Grabbing her hips, I pushed her against the door until it clicked, trapping the hanger's hook—and my wife.

"Spread your legs."

She did as she was told, my hands hovering protectively near her in case she lost her balance. It was a fucking beautiful sight. My pregnant wife, legs spread, her nude, curvy body stretched and on display.

"You are the sexiest thing I've ever laid eyes on," I muttered, almost annoyed. Soon, I'd have to go without her for far too long. The thought of her being physically kept from me after the baby was born was nearly enough to make me want her to stay pregnant forever.

"Prove it," she challenged.

I'd learned that if I wasn't dominating Belle, I could never quite expect how she'd react in the bedroom. Sometimes, she folded into submission without prompting, a sign that she needed my dominance. Others, she met each bite and mark with her own teeth and nails. And then there were times like tonight, when her sharp tongue spurred me on, reminding me of the reason I'd never been able to resist it.

The reason I never would be able to resist her.

Those were the nights she came the most.

I moved my hand between her legs, pressing my palm to her warm pussy. She moaned, trying to open her legs wider. I chuckled at her obviousness. Despite her impatience, I rewarded her by sliding my hand farther and pushing my thumb past her wet slit to rest on her swollen clit. She groaned as I circled it.

I'd start slow and work her until she couldn't keep her eyes open. I coaxed the orgasm from her gently. There was no need to rush. She was always the most beautiful as her body wound around me—around whatever I was giving her—and I wanted to enjoy watching her until every inch of her was taut and strained and mine.

She pulled against the hanger, moaning, and I crushed my mouth to hers, stealing those sweet sounds from her lips. I increased the pressure, dipping one finger inside her and then another. I stroked the pleasure out with slow, deliberate fingers until there was nothing left of her to wind up.

And then I let her go. Belle unraveled around me with a strangled cry, her limbs seizing and then delicately shuddering to a tremble like butterfly wings.

I gave her a moment before I took the next orgasm from her. By the time we were nearing the third, she was gasping and straining.

"Something wrong, beautiful?" I asked smugly.

"I want your cock." The request fell so wantonly from her lips—I had to grant it.

I withdrew my hand, earning an amusing pout from her. I ignored it and unhooked her from the armoire.

Sex was trickier these days, but not impossible—and I loved a challenge. Guiding her to the bed, her hands still tied, I bent her over it, arms stretched above her head. Her fingers grabbed the bed cover. I loved it when she braced for impact.

"Fuck me, sir," she said as I moved between her legs, biting out the addition.

"That feels like an order." I rubbed the tip of my cock along her swollen sex. She was already near the point of climax. One touch would push her over the edge. I backed away and she cried out.

"Do you feel how ready you are?" I asked. "I could blow on your clit and you would come. You only get one chance to get this right, beautiful. One brush of my finger or my tongue? A kiss? How do you want me to break you?"

"Give me your cock," she begged, "sir."

"Fuck, I could never deny you that."

I resisted the urge to slam inside her. I was so ready to feel her milking my dick that it took more than a fair amount of self-control. I wanted to enjoy every moment of her climax. I stood behind her stroking my shaft. Her head shifted, straining to see what I was doing.

"I want to come with you," I told her, moving so she could watch me jack off. I jerked my dick slowly but roughly until a bead of ejaculation formed. Belle whimpered, knowing she was about to get what she wanted, and I couldn't help myself.

I brushed it off with my thumb, leaned over, and offered it to her. She took it, sucking it clean with wild eyes. If I wasn't about to come that would have been all I needed. I grabbed her hips, guiding my throbbing dick inside her. She began to come as soon as I breached her and so I took my time, giving her pleasure inch by inch until she burst as I buried myself inside her and released.

This was how it was with us. I wanted her like it was the first time—everytime. I took her like it was the last time—everytime.

After, I laid awake and watched her sleep again. It was becoming a bad habit, but I couldn't ignore the dread I felt every time I closed my eyes—every time I took my eyes off her.

8

BELLE

The baby was never coming out of me. I was going to be the first woman in history to be pregnant for years. Despite Smith's ambitious lovemaking, I hadn't felt so much as a contraction yet. The doctor had been no help. She simply told me what the internet did: walk, have sex, wait. So I pulled past the gates of Buckingham, parked my car in the farthest space from the living quarters and heaved myself out of the seat of my Mercedes. Smith was put out that I wouldn't take the Range Rover, but I would be consigned to it soon enough. I wanted to enjoy the last little freedoms of life as long as I could. The sight of me huffing my way towards the palace, temporarily stunned a Beefeater in the middle of a ceremonial shift change enough that he stopped in his tracks before remembering his duty and snapping back to attention. I didn't know whether to be offended that I'd managed to distract a trained guard or proud.

Georgia met me at the entrance of Buckingham with a smile, which I immediately found suspicious. She'd been getting along a lot better with Clara, but that friendliness hadn't exactly carried over to our relationship. I couldn't help feeling that somehow she disapproved of Smith marrying me, although I had no idea why. I was the best thing that ever happened to him. I considered telling her this, but settled for a simple, breathless, "Hello."

"Should I get a wheelchair or something?"

"Hilarious," I said in a flat tone. "I'm trying to get some exercise in, so this diva will get the hell out of me. And that's pretty impossible since I'm not allowed to go anywhere thanks to you."

"Me?" She snorted, flicking a lock of hair over her shoulder as she led me towards Clara's private residence. "That's all your husband, sweetheart."

"You're enabling him," I said grumpily. I'd thought Smith handled the situation at the baby shower better than expected—until the following morning when I discovered Brexton Miles was my new shadow. It could be worse. He was funny and sweet and built like a tank. But any hopes I had of scurrying around London, enjoying my last hurrah, were dashed by his presence. I felt like I had a babysitter.

"You lucked out. You got Brex. Your best friend is stuck with me," Georgia said as she opened the door.

"It's terrible," Clara called from her sitting room. William was on her lap, gurgling happily. She'd put him in a pair of short pants that matched his blue eyes. A sweep of black hair stuck up on top of his head, making him look more like his father everyday. "She doesn't even like to shop."

"Neither do you," I reminded Clara. She really had changed. It hit me every day that I came here, and I'd been here most days since our return from Sussex. Not only did she live in the heart of London and wave from the balcony for state events and host garden parties on the lawn, she was a wife and a mother.

"I like buying tiny baby things," she admitted with a wink. "I can't help it. It makes me happy."

Happiness was something that seemed to be in perpetually short supply around here of late. Clara and Alexander adored each other—anyone could see that. But their love came with its own problems. Loving him had proven to be nearly deadly for her in more ways than one. Little William, sitting on her lap now the picture of health, had already required surgery for a heart defect in his short life. Money and power might have bought them guards and security, but it couldn't protect them from fate. Nothing could.

Clara stood, lifting William higher on her shoulder, and nodded toward the nursery.

"That's my cue," Georgia said, holding up a tabloid. "I'll be in here, learning the Royal Family's most devastating secret."

"Be sure to let me know what it is later," Clara told her, and they shared a laugh. I did my best not to stare at them like they were aliens. Something twisted in my chest, and it took a moment for me to recognize what it was: jealousy.

They'd bonded. Of course, they had after everything Clara had been through and how much time they spent together. It wasn't that I wanted to be closer to Georgia. Somehow I was certain we'd always lock horns. But I missed the days of living with Clara, gossiping over too much wine, thinking the biggest decision I had to face was what flowers to carry for my wedding. That had been before Alexander and Smith and the insane world we found ourselves in now.

As soon as we entered William's room, Elizabeth rushed

over, grabbed my hand, and dragged me down to her own room. "I have a new tea set."

She still lisped as she spoke and my heart leapt. I didn't bother to remind her that I had given her the tea set for her birthday a month ago. It hardly seemed important. Elizabeth pretended to pour both of us cups, and I took mine, sipping daintily to her delight. A few years from now, she'd be here with my daughter, playing together. I almost couldn't wait.

If Smith didn't keep us locked away in Sussex, that was.

She laid a tiny warm hand on my stomach, scrunched her nose, and said, "Kick!"

"I'm not sure she'll do it on command, darling," I warned her.

She turned a look so purely Alexander on me that I couldn't help but giggle, which resulted in a kick, after all.

After a few minutes, I finally managed to convince Elizabeth to return to William's room.

"My room is more interesting," she informed me, only missing about half the syllables as she spoke. "We should stay here."

"I want to see your brother, too." I suspected she might be a little jealous herself.

"Fine." She shrugged. "But he's boring."

Judging from the scene that greeted me when we finally made our way back into the nursery, William had ceased being boring and finally done something interesting.

"Clever boy," Clara cooed, camera trained at him while he stuck his toes in his mouth.

We stepped inside and his head turned, sensing the movement—and then he rolled over.

"Oh!" I clapped, feeling as though I'd won the lottery.

Elizabeth looked up at me before joining in. I guessed even she was impressed by this milestone.

Clara straightened up, letting Wills do his tummy time, and smiled but I caught her eyes wandering over me like she expected I might burst any moment. "I wasn't sure we'd see you today."

"I'm going to serve the baby a vacate notice." I waddled over to the chair across from her and lowered into it, feeling instant relief. "I feel as big as a house."

"You look gorgeous." I could tell she meant it, which made the compliment stick even if I was feeling about as attractive as hippopotamus.

"I'm just ready to meet this little one." I rubbed the spot where she'd been kicking me moments earlier.

Clara looked at her phone, her eyes flickering over the video. I heard myself exclaim and clap. She swiped something and sighed.

It was clear she'd sent the video to her husband, but that wasn't who she was thinking of. I knew because I'd been worrying about Edward, too. "You should send it to him."

"Alexander hates missing this stuff."

"You know what I meant." I'd seen the pain in her eyes when she'd realized he wasn't coming to the baby shower last week. I'd nearly called him the next day to give him a piece of my mind, upset that he'd missed it, especially since Alexander hadn't been there. I'd had to remind myself that I needed to give him the space to heal, even if I wanted to mother him until he felt better.

"Have you spoken with him?" she asked with some hesitation.

"For a few minutes." I'd only seen him once since we

came back to London, and no part of me wanted to relay to her the things he'd said that day. I knew that if I told her we'd lunched together, she would ask and I would have to lie more. Edward had asked me not to tell her how much he was struggling with his feelings toward his family. I needed to respect that as much as I could. "He called to tell me he was going to Italy."

"Italy?" She did a decent job of looking surprised, but Edward had been running away as often as possible from the city. I didn't have the heart to tell her he planned to be gone for the holidays, as well.

"He said he's eating all the pasta and getting fat." He had, in fact, used those exact words.

But Clara's voice was distant, lost to guilt, when she responded, "He's never going to forgive me."

"It's not you that he has to forgive," I said gently. "He needs time to process what David did and what..."

I stopped before I brought up Alexander. Truthfully, I was sure he'd had a choice. I knew what Smith would have done in the same situation. He'd kill anyone that hurt his family without hesitation—even if it was someone he cared about. But that didn't make David's death or how it happened any easier to swallow. We could only hope that someday the brothers would find a way to move past the tragedy.

"He'll come back," I said, needing to believe it. Everyone deserved a second chance. No matter what they'd done. "Send him the video."

She thought about it a moment before she pulled up the video and sent it. When she was done, she laid the phone on a side table and reached down to pick up Wills, who'd begun to fuss on the floor. "So, no induction?"

"I asked," I said, feeling my frustration creep back up. "She said it's not recommended without medical necessity. I told her I was going crazy but, apparently, that's not enough of a reason."

"Trust me, you don't want a c-section," Clara said, smiling in a way I'd come to expect from a mother who'd already experienced the blessed event of childbirth. "Maybe there's something you and Smith could do..."

"Believe me, we've tried."

"I figured," she said sympathetically.

"Of course, he's treating me like I'm fragile. Maybe that's why it's not working."

Clara bit her lower lip, glancing over at Elizabeth who was busily pulling books off William's shelves. "Prefer something a bit darker?"

"Rougher, at least." I rolled my eyes. "I could really use a break, but I think he's worried that he'll take things too far."

"That's what safe words are for."

I flinched in surprise. Clara and I had danced around the particulars of our sex lives for years now, but we both knew we were dealing with dominant men. Still, given that she'd once blushed at the mention of missionary position, I couldn't help being a bit shocked to hear her using a term like that.

"Don't look shocked," she said. "I found a collar in your closet once."

I sighed at the reminder of how much things had changed.

"Tell him you want it like that," she advised me, seeing the disappointment on my face. "Remind him that a little kink isn't going to hurt the baby."

"I just need a break," I admitted to her.

"Do you want to talk about what happened?" she asked gently.

Talking wasn't going to solve this. I'd tried that already, but I couldn't deny Smith had a right to be worried. "There's nothing to talk about. I have six feet of imposing black man following me around."

"Brex is sweet though," she said, "and hot."

"I knew you thought he was hot," a deep voice cut in. Clara's eyes closed tightly, embarrassed to be caught by her husband. "He'll be so pleased."

She swiveled in her seat like a top, a look of horror dashing across her face. "You are not going to tell him!"

"I won't," he said with a smirk. "But I'm not the one he's babysitting these days."

Clara turned pleading eyes on me. "Don't tell him."

"No promises," I said, laughing despite myself.

"What are you doing here?" Clara demanded. "Sneaking up on me? Shouldn't you be running the country?"

"Apparently, I should be concerned that my wife finds one of my best friends hot." But, for once, he looked anything but. The truth was that Clara only had eyes for him, and he only had eyes for her. As different as my marriage was from theirs, I recognized the total adoration they had for one another. I'd experienced it myself.

"Go back to being king. This is girl time."

"I came to do this." He leaned down and placed a lingering kiss on her mouth that lasted just long enough that I found myself staring. When he broke away, she gazed wistfully at him as he leaned down to kiss Wills on the forehead. "And to tell my son, I was proud of him. But now I have to get back. Very busy running the country and such."

"Sure," Clara said dryly.

"I'll see you in a few hours," Alexander said huskily, and a knot inside me tightened. I really was going to have to push Smith to be a little more demanding tonight.

When he finally left, Clara watched the door for a few seconds before clearing her throat. "What were we talking about?"

"My hot bodyguard," I reminded her, and she winced.

"New subject," she said. "Not that it matters, because he's completely in love with Georgia."

"Georgia?" I repeated.

Clara looked as though this was old news. "Head over heels. I think she loves him, too, but she won't let herself be with him."

I thought of Smith and how broken he was when we first met. "Maybe she just needs time."

But we both knew it wasn't a matter of time. We'd both had whirlwind romances when we'd found the right person. Suddenly, I found myself feeling sad for Brex, who'd put up with all my sass and brought me a chocolate biscuit for breakfast. And Clara was right, he was hot. "What exactly is she waiting for? I don't think guys get more perfect."

"I think love is a lot like finding the right key," Clara said as though she'd given this some thought. "When it comes to the heart, more than one key might fit, but only the right one unlocks it." She shook herself out of her dreamy haze, frowning when she saw my pout. "What?"

I sighed before sheepishly confessing, "Now, I'm just thinking about handcuffs."

9

SMITH

I showed myself into the King's study, knowing full-well that it would likely be enough to have my security clearance revoked. Taking a seat in an upholstered wingback, I had to admit I appreciated Buckingham's sense of tradition where comfort was concerned. The fire flickering in the hearth made the room feel rather homey. It certainly lessened the sense of formality and occasion that accompanied more public meetings with the young King. I had been here a number of times and knew my way around the space. I also knew that Alexander would be returning from his audience with the Prime Minister shortly. I'd been working with Alexander up until a few weeks ago. It wasn't that we were on poor terms. Our relationship was almost entirely transactional and always had been. I'd come to him with information regarding his father's death. At the time, I'd only wanted to see Hammond put behind bars, so I could finally claim my life as my own. But the situation had proven more complicated than either of us had foreseen.

Alexander paused in the doorway, his clear eyes

narrowing dangerously when he spotted me sitting next to his fire. He closed the door to his office, moving to his desk without so much as a word.

"I asked for a meeting," I said by way of explanation.

"One usually waits for said meeting to be scheduled." He shuffled a few papers around before giving up the ruse of being too busy to join me. Still, his lips turned down as he walked over to a brass cart and poured himself a bourbon. He held up the crystal decanter in offering.

I shook my head. "I'm on call."

"The baby," he said knowingly. "Clara keeps her phone on all the time."

"I'm certain Belle appreciates that."

"Of course, your wife is here nearly every day, or has been for the last week. I imagine she might go into labor here."

"Is that a problem?" I asked, keeping my tone even. Being near Alexander meant constantly recalculating my position.

"No." He took a sip thoughtfully before taking the chair opposite mine. "But if she's here, I'm not certain she needs my best man nannying her."

"Need I remind you that you owe me?" I said coolly. Alexander did not want me as an enemy. Perhaps, he needed a reminder of that fact.

"I know that, but I can't say I appreciate you reassigning men on my behalf." He crossed one leg over the other, unbuttoned his navy jacket and relaxed into the seat.

"Let's cut the bullshit, shall we?" I offered. "Where's my father's gun?"

"In a safe in this very office." His eyes stayed trained on me. A lesser man might have looked toward wherever this safe was hidden, but, as strained as my relationship to him was, I knew Alexander was no small man. He'd proven time and again that he was willing to go as far as he needed to in order to protect his family. I could respect that.

I simply didn't have to sacrifice the safety of my own family for his, though.

"Are you sure?"

"Clara told me about the present you received. I checked the gun that night," he told me. "It's still loaded, Smith."

I sucked in a deep breath, wishing I could get that drink after all. For the most part, I'd given up alcohol in recent years, but I couldn't claim sobriety. Still, I'd managed to keep my drinking mostly to social occasions and not as a form of escape. Now wasn't the time to change that habit.

"I don't suppose it's a coincidence," Alexander admitted. His gaze traveled to the fire where it lingered for an unnaturally long time before he spoke again. "Georgia mentioned that you saw it as connected to MI-18."

"Don't you?" I asked.

"I struggle to see anything as unconnected from them these days," he said bitterly. "To be honest, when I heard you were moving your family to Sussex, I was relieved."

I blinked, processing this confession. Alexander had seemed cold at best when I'd informed him that I wanted to step away from future investigations. I'd helped him before because losing Clara would have broken parts of my wife that would never heal, and because I sympathized with Alexander's situation. If it were me, I'd want his help. But we had more to lose than ever before—and I was more than a little surprised to hear that he recognized that.

"But now you're back in the city," he continued.

"We aren't staying."

"Does your wife know that?" he asked in a soft voice that was uncharacteristically concerned. "Because she seems to be clinging to her life here rather tightly."

"That will change."

He inclined his head as though he understood that all too well. "In the meantime, Brex will remain nearby. No one will get past him, but if you do decide—"

"Once we're out of London, I can handle matters," I cut him short. Alexander owed me one, and I would call in that favor, but part of starting over meant severing ties.

"It won't be easy for her," Alexander warned me. "Clara relies on her. I've seen what losing Edward has done to my wife. I imagine she'll reach out to Belle more, but I'll do what I can to ease the transition."

"In the meantime," Alexander said, rising from his chair, "would you like your father's gun back?"

I knew what he was asking. It wasn't a simple offer to return the weapon I'd left in his safekeeping. He was asking how far I was willing to go to protect her. I'd made a choice the day I'd given him that gun. I'd chosen then to believe we'd found our way out of the darkness, but the clouds had returned to block the sun once more. Our eyes locked, an unspoken understanding passing between us. The two of us might not always see eye to eye but we both agreed on one thing. When it came to our wives, we would sacrifice anything to keep them safe.

"Please."

Alexander moved to his desk, reaching under, his hand hidden from sight. A moment later, a portrait of his father opened slowly. I watched as he opened the safe, which was locked with a biometric sensor. He reached inside and withdrew the handgun. Instead of handing it to me, he pushed open the chamber and took out the copper bullet. He held it up between his thumb and forefinger for me to see.

"A word of advice, this isn't about him. Whatever happens now, it's bigger than that. You can't let the past cloud your judgement. You can't let ghosts distract you from the real enemy."

Like he had. He didn't have to say it. Alexander had trusted the wrong people and nearly lost everything. It was a mistake he didn't want to see repeated. I nodded, and Alexander slipped the bullet into his own pocket.

"You don't need that," he told me, passing me the gun.

It wasn't a call to pacifism. It was a reminder to focus on the danger in front of me, and whoever was behind that had already sent me the ammunition that would end this.

"If you need more," Alexander offered.

"I'll be in touch." But we both knew that wasn't true. The next time I left London it would be for good.

10

BELLE

Clara had put ideas in my head. I'd spent the afternoon stewing over what she said. Smith was my key. He fit me in every way. Between the stress of remodeling, running a business, and a seemingly never ending string of threats to both us and our friends, we never seemed to catch a break. It wasn't as though our sex life had suffered, but I finally understood what was missing. Smith was being a gentleman, preparing for the moment he would become a father.

I loved him for that. Despite his own tragic childhood, he'd wanted a baby as much as I did. Maybe more. He had faith in our ability to be good parents, which made me feel a bit more calm about it as her arrival approached. Nothing had escaped his notice from foot rubs to snacks to coming with me to the doctor. He was falling into the role with an ease I almost envied.

But one of the ways he fit me the most was by being rough and unexpected. I would also want to make love to my husband, but sometimes I wanted him to fuck me.

Like he owned me.

Because he did.

Like I craved it.

Because I did.

In the beginning of my pregnancy, especially after losing our first baby, I'd appreciated his gentle concern. But there was no cause for concern. Every scan had shown a completely healthy baby. I'd flown through this pregnancy with nothing to worry about, save for a little morning sickness in the first trimester. I'd seen Clara's body during a doctor's appointment when she was pregnant with William. Alexander hadn't held back. He'd marked her as his own.

I never thought I'd have to ask Smith to do the same to me. But more than ever I craved the liberation his total dominance gave me. I needed him to take me, use me, possess me.

Basically, I was horny as hell.

It might have been building up the whole time. Maybe it was last minute hormone fluctuations. Part of me even knew it might be down to the uncertainty of what to expect after she was born. Would we ever get a minute alone? What if he didn't want me the same way he did now? What if everything changed? I wanted to believe it wouldn't, but a last hurrah of a more erotic nature seemed in order, to be safe.

On our way back to the townhome, I turned to Brex. "Can we stop in Mayfair?"

He glanced at me and nodded. "Sure. Anywhere in particular?"

"Just down Grosvenor." I didn't bother telling him what I was up to. Brex was generally a good sport. He didn't fuss when I insisted on sitting in the front of the Range Rover with him. Smith had flat-refused to allow him to drive me in the Bugatti, which in fairness, was nearly impossible for me to get into and out of at this stage. But even if I couldn't fit behind the steering wheel, I wasn't going to treat Brex like my driver. It was bad enough to have a bodyguard. It was worse when he was part of your social circle. At least, he felt that way to me. Smith, as usual, treated him like an outsider.

The first bars of a song started playing on the Rover's radio and I arched an eyebrow in surprise. "I didn't peg you for liking country music."

"I don't as a rule," he admitted, flashing a sheepish smile that was at odds with his intimidating presence. "The singer is my cousin. He just won some award or something."

Brexton Miles, my bodyguard and one of the King's right hand men, a man who'd been to war, a man you called in to handle deadly situations, was secretly a giant teddy bear. I found myself thinking about what Clara said about him being in love with Georgia. I couldn't see that working out.

"Well, in that case." I turned up the song. "It's not bad."

"I'll tell him it meets your approval." He turned off the A4202 onto Grosvenor, passing a number of shops on his way. There'd been a time when Grosvenor Park had housed numerous embassies. Many of them were now being converted into luxury flats to service the affluent locals. We passed the Eaton Mayfair, a luxurious Georgian building turned hotel where one of my favorite restaurants was located. My stomach rumbled, an increasing phenomenon. I seemed to always be hungry these days. But I wasn't looking for food now. I had something else on my mind.

"Here!" I said as soon as I spotted the lacquered black storefront. It stood out against the stone and brick of the surrounding buildings. But it wasn't merely the paint choice that contrasted with the high-end watch shop across the street or the chic clothing store next door, it was its window. My favorite lingerie shop did little to hide its intentions. Mannequins sported sensual lace that snaked and crossed in fashions as provocative as its name implied.

Brex took one look at it and swallowed hard. "I'll wait outside."

Despite my refusal to be driven around, he had the advantage of being more mobile than me. Before I'd managed to unbuckle myself by my overdue baby bump, he'd circled round to open my door. He helped me out with a patient smile.

"I'll only be a moment." I flashed him a shy smile. I don't know why I was so embarrassed. If Clara was right and he was in love with Georgia, he was going to need to be a little less prim in the face of some leather and lace.

Stepping inside, I immediately knew I'd made the right choice. Inside, the store turned into a glamorous and darkly decadent space. Black carpet with a subtle floral pattern and gold shelving maintained the hedonistic atmosphere. I might not fit into most of the items in the shop at the moment. I couldn't help admiring a body suit of intersecting straps that formed a sexy cage on one mannequin's torso. Someday, I'd be able to wear something like that for Smith again. For now, my choices were limited to the store's more suggestive accessories.

"May I help you?" A shop girl wandered over, and I felt a surge of envy at her tiny waist. She could fit into anything here and I could barely undo my safety buckle in the car.

Turning from the glass case of gold collars and bracelets, I smiled at her. Her mouth fell open, confirming that I was as big as a house.

"I won't pop," I promised.

"My apologies!" She sounded sincere but dubious as to the veracity of my claim. "You didn't look..." A ruddy blush painted her cheeks as she stopped herself.

I bit back a giggle, marveling that my pregnant belly could shock anyone in a store full of crystal-tipped whips, gold-plated handcuffs, and lingerie that served no other purpose than to entice.

"Can I see that one?" I managed to say evenly, pointing to a simple collar made from gold and black, silk rope.

She unlocked the case and withdrew it for my inspection. "It's a lovely piece." She sounded less embarrassed and more impressed. "That's a slipknot, if you slide it, you can adjust the collar."

She reached to demonstrate how the cold collar split in half when the silk rope was loosened, allowing it to slip over one's head.

"Would you like to try it?" She held it out.

"I don't know if my husband would appreciate someone else putting a collar on me."

Her eyes widened, flashing to my belly and back up. "I'm s-s-sorry."

I was going to give the poor girl a heart attack if I didn't stop playing with her. It had been a long time since I shocked someone, and I couldn't help enjoying it a little.

"I'll take it."

"Would you like it gift-wrapped?" she asked with a nod.

"There's an idea," I said thoughtfully. The piece would send the message, but a gift like total submission deserved the proper presentation. I wasn't about to bother strapping myself into one of their sexier pieces. I didn't need to either. True sensuality lay in the suggestion of what was to come. I walked over to a display of silky kimonos.

Out of the corner of my eye, a blue dressing gown caught my attention. Its sheer silk-crepe flowed elegantly on the hanger, its loose silhouette punctuated by delicate, black lace. "And I'll take this. Please don't crease it."

"Of course." She bustled off to ring up my purchases, leaving me to look longingly at the rest of the shop.

A few moments later, I stepped out clutching two pink shopping bags. Brex opened my door, taking the bags to stow in the back.

As we approached Holland Park, he cleared his throat. "Will you be needing me this evening?"

I suspected that no matter what I said someone would be keeping an eye on our home for the night. I'd taken to inviting Brex for dinner just to punish Smith for making the decision to bring in outside security without my consent.

"Take the night off," I told him brightly. I was going to be occupied. "We'll order in."

"As you wish." He looked on the verge of laughter when we finally pulled to the front of our house. Smith wasn't home yet, so Brex accompanied me inside. He swept each room for any signs of intrusion and checked the security feeds while I found myself nibbling on leftover cake from my baby shower. Spontaneous eating of cake ranked fairly high on my list of pregnancy perks.

"Everything looks good," he informed me.

I held up the platter of petit-fours from the fridge. "Want one?"

He swiped one and hitched a thumb toward the door. "I'll stick around until Smith gets home, but maybe I should..."

"Thank you." At least, he knew how to read the room.

After Brex stepped out, I finished my treat, placed an order for curry from a spot around the corner to arrive in a few hours. Then, I went upstairs to get ready. Removing a box from each bag, I untied the black ribbon securing them and lifted their lids. Checking my phone, I discovered a message from Smith. He'd be home soon, giving me just enough time to freshen up.

I laid out the robe and collar before shucking off my clothes. Checking the mirror, I found my hair and make-up only needed a little help. I applied a fresh coat of red lipstick and spritzed a hint of perfume on my wrist. I didn't really need to do more.

I'd told the shopgirl that my husband wouldn't appreciate anyone else collaring me, but he was going to have to make an exception tonight. I couldn't wait for him to do it, because I wanted to present myself to him as a gift but also as a reminder that I belonged to him, completely and utterly.

Sliding the knot down, I loosened the collar until I could easily slip it over my head. Then, I carefully tightened it, leaving two lengths of black rope hanging between my breasts. I felt a warm surge of arousal between my legs as I thought of him grabbing hold of the rope like a leash. I was drawing the sheer robe over my shoulders when I heard the front door open and Smith's voice carry through the otherwise empty house.

"Beautiful?"

I bit my lip, tying the belt of the dressing gown, loosely under my breasts, allowing it to hang open enough that the collar was properly displayed. I wasn't nude, but not an inch of me was covered. I moved into the hall swiftly, padding quietly on bare feet as he called out for me again. I heard his shoes on the bottom step just as I reached the top of the staircase.

"I've been..." his words died on his lips.

"I'm sorry, Sir," I simpered. "I should have come more quickly."

He kept staring until I raised an eyebrow. Then he took the steps two at a time until he was close enough to reach for me. He stopped there, his fingers dancing over the silk robe hanging between my breasts in invitation.

"Come quickly?" he repeated. "It's too late for that, beautiful. I think I'll take my time."

"About that," I purred. "Take your time, but don't be gentle."

"Belle," he said, his voice pitching slightly with alarm, but I saw his eyes darken. He craved this as much as I did.

I placed my index finger over his sculpted lips before he could raise an objection. "We've made love every day since we found out I was pregnant. Tonight I need you to fuck me. Own me. Show me I belong to you."

"You've always belonged to me," he growled.

"Prove it," I said in a low voice.

His head tilted. "Are you sure..."

"Do you want me on my knees?" I asked. "Do you want me to beg?"

His tongue flicked over his lower lip, and I knew that part of him did. But he shook his head.

I swallowed the scream of frustration trying to escape me.

"I will," I threatened. "I will get down on this floor and beg until you fuck me, Price."

He pressed his lips into a thin line. It took me a moment to realize that he wasn't upset. He was trying not to smirk. "I thought you wanted me to dominate you."

"Unbelievable!" I threw my hands in the air, stomping back toward our bedroom feeling the hot prickle of tears. I sank onto the end of the bed, burying my face in my hands so he wouldn't see me cry.

He didn't want me. Not like this. Not like he used to. That or he'd managed to harness a supernatural level of restraint he'd never possessed before. Smith could control himself. He could fuck me for hours if he wanted. But resist me? That hadn't been a possibility before.

"Go away," I said miserably as he stalked into the room, but the words had barely left my lips when his fist closed over the rope, yanking my face up as he bent to capture my mouth. There was nothing gentle about his kiss.

"I don't like it when you tell me how to play with you," he said, his voice as rough as his hands as he jerked me to my feet. "I'll play with you how I want to, beautiful, and you won't complain. You'll come when I demand it. You'll offer me your pretty ass to punish. Right fucking now."

I nearly came on the spot.

Smith loosened his hold on my leash only so I could turn.

"Bend over," he ordered. "Hold the bed."

I did as I was told. He slid the collar around so that the ropes were at the back of my neck. "If you can't breathe, you will say red."

I started to protest.

"Don't fight me on this or I'll fuck you until you're about to come and then stop and make you do it yourself while I watch." He bit my shoulder. "Understood?"

"Yes, Sir."

"That won't be a hardship for me," he warned. "Feeling you squirm and then watching you punish yourself. I might actually like it."

I whimpered. Part of me wanted to push him, so I could put on the show he described. I wanted to be his every fantasy, I always had. But tonight I wanted to be owned and marked.

He lifted my dressing gown over my hips and patted my rear. His palm slid over it. "Perfect. Well, almost."

I heard his hand whip through the air and then felt the crack as it collided with my soft flesh. Stinging heat seared through me, and I cried out.

"Now, it's perfect," he said appreciatively. He rubbed out the heat in the spot before delivering another smack. This continued until my skin sang without reprieve. "Your ass is so beautiful when it's red. I love seeing the marks of my fingers and palm on it, especially while I fuck you. Would you like me to do that now?"

I mumbled a yes. My neck jerked back as he pulled the rope.

"What was that, beautiful?"

"Please, Sir," I repeated more clearly, feeling a fresh rush of heat between my legs.

"First." He released me and walked to the front of the bed. Picking up a stack of pillows, he stuffed them under me, helping me fold my arms around them. "For leverage. Don't fight me on this. You two are the most precious things in the world to me."

I swallowed, holding the pillows tightly. He always took care of me. He saw to every need, even the ones I didn't know I had. And now, I was about to be his again. I bit back a sob when he moved behind me and positioned his dick against my seam.

"So fucking perfect," he muttered as he slammed into me.

My eyes closed. I became a blank space, my existence distilled to the anchor of his cock inside me. This was everything I needed, everything I would ever need.

11

SMITH

I prided myself on being calm in a crisis situation, but no one had warned me that child labor was not a crisis but a goddamn circus act. Despite having months to prepare, nothing seemed to be in place. Belle's bag wasn't in the designated spot, my mobile needed to be charged, and I couldn't get Edward on the phone.

"Wait," Belle commanded, stopping on the stairs suddenly. She grabbed the railing, her knuckles going white, as she hunched over and sucked in a breath so sharply, I thought she might collapse.

I pressed a hand to the small of her back, trying to remember what they'd taught us at the class we'd taken last month. Then, I'd filed away the information, wondering if it would be useful. Now? I realized the suggestions were nothing more than distractions, meant to keep me from seeing what an utterly pointless bastard I was. I'd gotten her into this mess, and there wasn't a damn thing I could do to be useful, except help her to the car—a task that was taking record amounts of time.

When she finally straightened, she shot me a tired smile. "That was a bad one."

"Let's get you in the car before another one hits, beautiful." I was beginning to worry we wouldn't make it to the hospital at the rate they were coming.

To her credit, Belle moved more quickly than I would in her state. Maybe she was concerned about the same thing. "Remember how I didn't want medication?" She whimpered as we reached the door. "I changed my mind."

"Soon," I promised. I kept a hold on her as I unlatched the door, kicking it open with my foot. Brex rushed up the steps, grabbing the bag. He carried a black umbrella to ward against a misty drizzle that had begun sometime after nightfall.

"You need more help?" he asked, having the poor timing to do so as another contraction started.

"Do. Not. Touch. Me," Belle said in a voice so thick with warning that Brex took a step away from her.

Brex and I exchanged looks. We'd stared down the barrel of guns. He'd gone to war. I'd throttled the life out of men. But neither of us had ever faced anything as terrifying as a woman in labor.

The car was blessedly warm, thanks to his foresight, and when Belle finally had another brief reprieve, I got her inside, said a prayer for the upholstery, and rounded to the driver's side. Brex didn't say anything as I slid behind the Range Rover's wheel.

"I'll follow."

I appreciated his escort. He'd been driving Belle around town the last few days but there was no one I would trust to see her to hospital at this moment. I pulled onto the road, grateful that she'd gone into labor in the night when the traffic was a trifle less congested. Still, the Rover handled differently than my car and I found my foot pressing the pedal to the floorboard, trying to get it to speed up. That coupled with wet pavement was a dangerous combination.

"We should have taken the Bugatti," I grumbled.

"I would have wrecked the seats." Between contractions, my wife was maintaining a relative sense of humor. I decided that was a good sign.

"Fuck the seats," I growled, missing the nimble sports car.

"I never thought I'd live to hear you say that," she said. Her hand fumbled over mine, but before I could weave my fingers through hers, she yelped and leaned forward.

"Fuck!" I drove through a traffic light, knowing full well it was red. A London cab slammed on its brakes as I swerved around it. The driver, a grandfatherly looking gentleman wearing a flat cap flipped the v's at me. I didn't bother to respond. Belle was going to have the baby in the car if we didn't get there soon.

In general, I disliked hospitals. I'd yet to have an experience in one that hadn't left me mourning a death or planning one. The last time I'd stepped foot inside one, Clara was giving birth. It had been a circus then, but tonight, St. Mary's was relatively calm from the outside. I'd never been so happy to see the Lindo Wing's private entrance.

"Did you call Clara?" Belle asked breathlessly as I pulled to park in front of the stone steps.

"I will, beautiful." By the time, I reached her side of the car to help her out, her eyes were narrowed into slits. "It's on the list! Edward and Clara, and then you need to let Lola know so she can be on call for Bless and—" She dissolved in a moan that sent alarm bells ringing inside me.

"It will all be handled." I rubbed her shoulders, waiting for it to pass, so that we could head inside. But this time when the contraction subsided, her annoyance remained.

"I can do it," she snapped, throwing off my hand as we made our way up the stairs and inside. Instantly, a nurse appeared with a wheelchair and Belle sank into it gratefully while I rattled off our particulars to her.

"Mr. Miles called us," she said, giving me a sympathetic smile that did nothing to soothe my fraying nerves.

"At least, he's thinking," Belle said grumpily, rubbing her stomach.

I'd no idea what to expect when she finally went into labor. I was prepared to take anything she threw my way, but I hadn't honestly expected her to be so put out with me so early on in the process.

"The midwife is going to examine you," the nurse told her. "Do you have other birth attendants coming?"

"Do I?" Belle looked to me, her expression murderous.

In fairness, we'd never settled on whether or not she would want others there. She had herself thought it best to wait until it was time. I wasn't about to point that out to her, though. "I'll call Clara."

"We'll get settled, Daddy. Don't worry." The nurse lowered her voice. "This is all perfectly normal."

My wife didn't normally hate me, so I wasn't convinced of that.

I stepped away to place the phone call. Striding past the door of another open room, I spotted a man at his wife's side, comforting her through a contraction. It looked so peaceful that I found myself staring until a nurse hustled past, nearly bumping into me. I continued to the lobby, which due to the private nature of the wing, was completely empty.

I hadn't thought to take Belle's phone, which left me with Alexander's number. He answered on the second ring, which somehow spoke to the nature of our relationship as much as the man himself. It was nearly midnight, but his tone was hushed.

"Yes?" He got straight to the point. It was usually business between us.

"Belle's in labor. She wants Clara." I didn't bother to ask Alexander to request she come. If I had to break down the doors of Buckingham and drag the Queen away in my arms, I would. Not even he could stop me.

But Alexander didn't press for more information. He simply replied in a clipped tone, "We're on our way."

Then, he hung up.

I'd done the only thing she'd asked of me, and what's more the only thing she seemed to want me to do. I thought of the couple in the other hospital room, lovingly working through birth. I had no idea why my wife had decided she no longer wanted me here, and maybe, I'd pay for it, but there was no way I was going to let her push me away now.

I strode back to the room, already labeled with our names on the outside placard and burst inside. Belle had a plastic mask over her face and her eyes widened as she spotted me.

I rushed closer, peppering the midwife with questions as a nurse continued to take Belle's vitals.

"It's only laughing gas," she cut me off. "It will help her cope with the pain a little better. Your wife is pretty far into labor."

"That's good news?" I looked to her for confirmation. I'd

never been the type of man to feel uncertain in a crisis, but this was new territory for me.

"It is, but that means she's in the worst of it now."

"How much longer?" I asked grimly.

"Minutes? Hours?" She shrugged, shoving her hands into the pocket of her burgundy scrubs. "Days?"

"Days?" Belle's voice piqued from the bed, and I looked over to see her staring dreamily at me from behind the mask.

"That's the gas," the midwife warned. "If she takes it off, it wears off instantly."

I took advantage of the situation. The prickly version of Belle had been replaced by a drowsy, but calm one. As I reached her, her eyes slammed close and her hand shot out, searching for mine. I hated to see her in pain, but I was grateful that she seemed to not just tolerate my presence, but want it. My eyes skipped to the second hand of my watch, timing how long this one lasted. The midwife was right. Things were definitely picking up speed. When the pain waned, she collapsed against the bed, her hand clutching her mask like it was life support. Her eyes fluttered.

"You should rest between contractions," the nurse advised her. "Soon, you won't be able to."

Belle turned bleary eyes on me.

"I'll be right here, beautiful," I promised.

"Clara?" she asked in a muffled voice.

She might no longer hate me, but I still wasn't the one she wanted. I forced a tight smile and nodded, reminding myself that I would do anything to help her through this—even leave if that's what she wanted. "She's on her way. It shouldn't take long."

Belle's hand withdrew from mine, and suddenly, she felt a million miles away.

"I'll go find them," I said, leaning over to kiss her forehead. "Rest."

She was in good hands. I had to trust that. But I couldn't shake the fear that everything was about to change—forever.

12

BELLE

The door opened and the comforting sight of Clara's face appeared. Her dark hair was swept into a messy bun and her cheeks were flushed. "May I come in?"

If I was willing to let go of the nitrous oxide I would have lunged at her. Instead, I had to settle for waving her frantically to my side. I was perfectly aware that I'd become a first class bitch sans pain reliever, and I couldn't bear the thought of lashing out at her, too. I'd already scared Smith off. The memory of his face when I'd snapped at him swam to mind, and it took me a second to realize I was blinking back tears.

"Oh, darling, what's wrong?" Clara raced to my side, grabbing my hand. So many things had changed in the last few years, but she was here, in a pair of jeans and a t-shirt, looking nothing like the Queen. She was just my best friend, and the person I needed to see more than anyone else in the world.

"I can't do this." The mask muffled my confession somewhat, but Clara's eyes melted with sympathy.

"You can. I know. They tell you it's terrible, but it's *really* terrible, isn't it?" She smiled and squeezed my hand. "But you get the most wonderful prize at the end."

"It's worth it?" I arched an eyebrow. For the first time, I was really beginning to wonder if I'd lost my mind. Why on earth had I thought I wanted to do this?

Clara's laughter tinkled like chimes. "I had a second one, didn't I?"

But it wasn't just the pain that had me scared. It was awful, and I'd never been so properly happy to be in a hospital before. But that came and went. Like Clara said, once this was all over, I would have a prize.

I would have a baby.

"I'm not ready," I croaked before I lost my nerve.

"Belle," Clara said without a hint of reproach, shaking her head. "That's not true."

"I'm not," I said, feeling panicked, despite the laughing gas. I pulled the mask off, so I could make my point more clearly and was rewarded with a contraction that sucked the air out of me.

Clara leaned closer, holding my hand tightly. "You've got this. It will only last another minute. Okay, thirty seconds. Almost over. There."

Her countdown had the remarkable effect of making the contraction feel less terrible than the others.

"Thank you," I said, grateful she was here.

"See? You're going to be fine."

"Maybe for this part!" My panic came roaring back, settling like a lump on my chest. "I have no idea what to do with a baby!"

"That's not true." Clara shook her head.

"I am not responsible enough to have a child."

"That's not true either."

"I'm going to be a horrible, selfish mother." This final admission of fear exploded out of me. I'd managed for months to keep it locked away in a deep, dark place. I'd walked around with it churning inside me all this time, and now, in the throes of labor, I didn't have the strength to keep it from spilling out.

"No," Clara said firmly, all the softness going out of her voice. She turned blazing eyes on me. "You are not going to be a horrible mother."

"How do you know that?" I sobbed, wanting more than anything to believe her, but it was impossible. There was only one reason that this fear had plagued me this long. It was the same reason I hadn't shared it with anyone.

It was true.

I knew it. Some women were cut out to be mothers. Clara was one of them. But the truth was that every time I went to visit her children—my god babies—I was more than happy to leave them behind with their parents at day's end. I never found myself missing them or wishing I could take them home. I couldn't do that with a baby of my own. It was one of the reasons I struggled with the idea of hiring a nanny. I should want to be a mum—all the time. Not just during non-working hours. But I couldn't imagine actually doing it. Worse, I couldn't imagine I'd be any good at it. "How do you know?" I repeated tearfully. "I don't want to move to the country or drive big cars or give up my company."

"Wanting things or not wanting them doesn't decide who you are as a person," Clara said softly. "And wanting a career and a baby doesn't mean you'll be a bad mom."

"Maybe I'm not meant to be a mother. Maybe—"

"You aren't her," Clara cut me off. "You aren't your mother."

It took me a second to process what she said. When it finally sunk in, I pulled the gas mask back over my face. I didn't have to let my anxiety and fear take control. I needed to calm down. Suddenly, I realized I'd let panic take hold of me.

"You've been worrying about this for months, haven't you?" she guessed. "Belle, you aren't your mother. I saw how she was the other night. I imagine that only made it worse, but the good news is that we aren't actually doomed to be our parents. Look at me. And Alexander."

And Smith, I thought. I hadn't wanted to tell him about my fears because I was worried that if he didn't feel the same way, I might plant the idea in his head. I closed my eyes, finally understanding why I hadn't been able to leash the raging bitch that had shown up on the way to the hospital.

"You think he still wants me to have his baby?" I asked flatly.

Clara grinned. "He looked like a ghost. He can't stand being apart from you."

"Yeah?" Maybe it was the nitrous, but I was starting to feel not only calmer, but a lot more prepared.

"Do you want me to get him?" she asked.

I opened my mouth to respond and doubled over, grabbing the tight ball my belly had become. The contraction lasted forever despite Clara's patient reminder that it would end eventually. When I finally caught my breath, she winked. "I think I better get him sooner rather than later."

I nodded. Maybe it would be minutes or hours or days still, but I knew one thing for sure. I wanted Smith by my side through all of it.

SMITH

I never thought I would look at anyone and find her as beautiful as Belle.

And then I met my daughter.

Her hair was so fine it looked like strands of silver that curled at her tiny ears. She was still pink from the vigorous rubdown the nurse had given her after birth. She hadn't been too pleased by that and had quickly demonstrated that she had my lung capacity. But once she'd been handed to Belle, she'd quieted immediately, looking to her with wide, searching eyes.

After Clara and Alexander had gone, I'd taken her so Belle could rest. I'd always known my wife was strong, but watching her bring life into the world proved even I'd underestimated the power inside her. I kept stealing glances at her while she slept, amazed that she'd chosen me to receive this gift.

She needed the sleep, and I'd been more than pleased to have the quiet time to study each of my daughter's tiny fingers. They wrapped around my index finger as she slept on my chest. How on earth could anything be so perfect? I felt like I'd known her my whole life, and like I couldn't wait to see who she would become. I was head-over-heels in love.

I'd been staring at her for an hour when Belle interrupted my reverie, "What do you think, Daddy?"

I carried the pink bundle over to her, carefully passing her to her mother. She woke with a squawk and immediately nuzzled her face against Belle's skin, searching for milk. Belle had never looked more perfect than when she had our daughter in her arms.

"Have you decided?" I asked Belle softly, not wanting to startle her.

Belle glanced up, confusion clouding her blue eyes before she smiled. "I guess I'm still tired. What am I deciding?"

"On her name, beautiful." I bit back a smile. I knew she was exhausted, and I couldn't blame her after what she'd gone through. "We can wait a little longer. I know we hadn't really narrowed them down."

There was no rush. Everything was perfect. We were exactly where we were meant to be, and for the first time, in as long as I could remember, I felt completely at peace. A week ago, we'd still been debating the question. Now it hardly seemed important. She was here with us.

Belle studied her silently, no doubt running through all the contenders in her mind. "Looking at her makes me feel like everything's going to be okay," she confessed. "I feel like our stars have changed."

"She's lucky, then." I couldn't help smiling. I had a feeling that we'd both landed on the same name. "Penny."

"Penny," she agreed in a soft voice. "Well, Penelope.

Sophia for the middle name. Penny might be lucky, but she should be wise, too."

"Penelope Sophia Price," I repeated. The baby yawned as I said it, her mouth drooping into a sleepy smile. "I think she approves."

"Speaking of, I hope you like this." I took a velvet box out of my pocket. I'd been carrying it for hours, waiting for the right moment to give it to her.

Belle's eyes narrowed on the satin bow tied around it. "What's that, Price?"

"I wanted to give you something special to remember the day our family became whole." I looked to my feet, wondering if she'd caught the break in my voice as I spoke. I'd never imagined I would be here now with the love of my life and our child. A life like that hadn't even been on my radar. Thank God, Belle had sauntered into my office. Thank God, I'd been unable to resist her smart mouth. That moment had led to this one.

"My hands are full," Belle whispered. "Could you?"

I nodded, slipping the bow off and opening the box to reveal the necklace inside. I'd found it at Harrods earlier this week and had been hiding it ever since.

"It's beautiful," she breathed. Belle turned teary eyes on me. "It's an opal—her birthstone."

"I'm glad she decided to finally come. I was getting nervous that I was going to have to take it back," I teased. I'm not certain I would have actually. The pendant's opal center, surrounded by diamonds, sparkled with a delicate rainbow of shimmering colors that somehow reminded me of the stars I'd promised her and the beauty we'd finally found after all we'd lost. The diamonds surrounding it, twisted at the top around one single, small pearl.

"The pearl..." I hesitated, suddenly unsure I should confess what the pearl had meant to me.

"Is for the baby we lost," Belle finished with a bittersweet smile. Of course she saw it, too. She hadn't talked much about the miscarriage while she was carrying Penelope, but I knew she still thought of the baby as much as I did.

"They're both with you," I said, my words thick on my tongue.

Belle leaned forward, and I brushed a few stray locks that had escaped her hair tie away from her neck before clasping the necklace around her.

"About the other decision," Belle said, her eyes never leaving our daughter.

"What other decision?" I wasn't sure how she could be thinking of anything but this moment. "Whatever it is, it can wait."

"No, it can't." There was a fierce edge to her words that reminded me of the lioness she'd been during birth. "I'm ready. As soon as they give the okay, I want to go home."

"The food isn't that bad." Actually, the tea service they'd delivered reflected the price tag that accompanied the ten-thousand pound birthing suite.

She finally looked up, her eyes locking with me. "I want to know she's somewhere safe."

"The security here—" I began.

"I'm not talking about here. Or London. When it's time to go, I want to go to Thornham," she said firmly. "I'm ready to go home."

14

SMITH

The crying started when Penny was three weeks old. We'd been warned to expect it by our doctors and the books Belle had read before her arrival, but I hadn't been prepared for what it would do to me. We'd returned to Thornham as soon as Belle was released from the hospital. I'd asked Georgia to pack up what remained of our things and send them to the estate. There had been tearful goodbyes with Clara and Aunt Jane. Edward hadn't returned from Italy, a fact which left a sour taste in my mouth. Mostly, because I kept searching for a reason why Belle suddenly seemed so distant from me. Three more weeks had passed, and the crying hadn't stopped.

At first, it had been easy to write off her aloofness as exhaustion. Penny slept as she pleased, preferring to nap during the day in our arms. We'd given up the idea of the nursery entirely, moving the bassinet to Belle's side of the bed within a few days of our return. That had worked for a while. I was more able to sleep through her newborn cries, so I took it upon myself to get up with her in the morning, so my wife could sleep. It was hard, but every time I looked into Penny's gray-blue eyes, I knew it was worth it. Belle slept better when I had the baby off in another room. But lately, she resisted waking up when Penny needed to nurse.

I told myself I couldn't blame her.

As the weeks passed, I found myself more aware of Penny's cries, waking more easily to help with midnight changes and feedings. Belle would nurse her, pass her back to me, and roll over to sleep. It wasn't that I minded. I didn't. It was that I wasn't sure if we'd simply developed a survival routine, so that we all got what we needed, or if we were going through the motions.

"Pictures in the morning," Belle murmured, sliding beneath the sheets and rolling toward the side of the bed where Penny had finally fallen asleep.

I turned to her, rubbing her thigh, and kissed her shoulder. "Are you sure you're up for it? Pictures can wait."

"We barely have time to send cards as it is," she said glumly. "We have a new house and a new baby. People will expect them."

"Who cares what they expect?" I said gently. She went rigid next to me.

"I can handle a simple task like Christmas cards," she snapped. Penny stirred, her whole body wiggling in its swaddle, and both of us froze. We'd grown used to holding our breath, worried that we'd accidentally woken her. When Penny remained asleep, Belle shifted slightly, so that my hand fell from her waist. "Good night."

I hesitated. Part of me wanted to clear this up. I hadn't meant to upset her. I'd only meant to remind her that we didn't need to worry about silly things like cards if it was going to make her more stressed out. But somehow I knew that stating so would only make matters worse. Instead, I settled for planting a kiss behind her ear. "Love you, beautiful."

She didn't respond. I told myself she'd already fallen asleep. She'd had a rough day. But I'd been telling myself that a lot lately, and I was having a hard time believing it myself. I laid next to her, staring at the ceiling, until sleep took me.

A mewling cry shattered the darkness and I rolled over, rubbing my bleary eyes. My hand reached to find Belle's side of the bed cold and empty. "Need help?"

The only response was Penny's cry. I sat up, instantly alert, flipping on the lamp on my nightstand. Belle sat on the edge of the bed, her head tilted toward the bassinet, one hand on its edge. At first, I thought she was rocking it, but neither she nor the bassinet moved. She must have fallen asleep like this, trying to get the baby back down. Penny grew more insistent, and I leapt up, circling the bed to the wicker bassinet. But when I reached it, I found Belle staring at the baby, her unblinking eyes rimmed with red from tears.

"Beautiful," I said gently, leaning to pick Penny up.

She startled slightly, finally lifting her face to mine. I took a step back when her eyes met mine. It was obvious she'd been crying but that wasn't what stunned me. I'd looked into her eyes a thousand times and known exactly what she was thinking: fear, excitement, joy. There was nothing there now. They were as void as a pool of still water at night.

I swallowed, worry pricking at the back of my mind. "Get some rest. I'll take her to the nursery for a bit."

She didn't respond. She only crept toward the pillow and rolled away from me, wrapping her knees to her chest. I paused, wondering if I should ask her to talk, but Penny began to cry and I spotted Belle's shoulders shake a little as she began to cry again. Stroking Penny's back and shushing her softly, I tiptoed from the room and closed the door behind me.

Penny continued to fuss as I carried her to the nursery, but a few minutes later, she settled in a sleepy bundle against my shoulder as I rocked her. If only I could soothe her mother as easily. The only thing that seemed to help Belle was when we weren't around.

Looking down at Penny, I marveled as her eyelids fluttered as she slept, sleepy smiles dancing on and off her face. I loved every moment she was in my arms—and I wanted Belle to feel the same way. I thought of her sitting on the edge of that bed and wondered how long she'd been there before I'd woken up. No matter how many times I told her to wake me or reminded her I was happy to get up with Penny, she never asked me to. She'd stopped asking me for much of anything. I loved her more than ever, and I'd never felt so disconnected from her. I wanted to make this right, but how do you make someone happy if you're what upsets them?

"Okay, can you lift the baby a little higher?" the photographer coaxed as I paced nervously around the sitting room. Belle obliged, holding Penny up under the arms as she gurgled. My wife and daughter were dressed as similarly as a grown woman and a six-week old could be. Penny in a cream top with a Peter Pan collar, navy short pants and a small bow. She's swept her hair up, pinning it into a twist. Between that and the cashmere sweater that draped elegantly off her shoulder, she looked like she'd stepped out of a magazine. "That's it. Now smile."

Belle's lips widened into a smile that I'd never seen before. It didn't belong to her. It was like looking at a stranger. She'd chosen to do the photos in front of our Christmas tree. Humphrey had overseen its erection and decorated it, a few days ago, at my request. Someday, the three of us would decorate our tree together and have our own traditions. This year, I didn't want to add any more chaos to our plates. The remodel had only finished last week despite having crews here around the clock—another sore point likely contributing to her stress. I'd been sure that as things settled down, Belle would finally feel at ease in our new home.

But the woman sitting in front of the Christmas tree was a stranger. An odd wave of protectiveness surged through me, and I fought the desire to take Penny out of her arms. It was unfair of me. Belle adored our daughter. That was clear. As often as I caught her crying, I found her rocking Penny to sleep, pure adoration written across her face.

"They're going to be terrible," Belle complained after the photographer had packed up and left. She shifted on her feet, swaying with Penny, who'd fallen asleep.

"No picture of the two of you could be terrible." I refused to even entertain the thought. Belle was the most perfect creature I'd ever seen, and our daughter already looked like a miniature version of her.

She opened her mouth to protest, but her mobile rang. I held out my arms and she passed Penny to me. I wandered the room as Belle took the call. We'd opted to keep many of the classic touches that showcased Thornham's history. It had cost a small fortune to rehab the room's crown moulding with its original swirls and flourishes. In the end, we'd opted to paint the entirety of the space a warm white which made the room feel open and airy—no small feat in a home of this age. To keep it from looking too modern, we'd opted for opulent velvet furniture in deep shades of blue and tables with rich, deep woodtones. The persian rug drew the entire space together and made it elegant and inviting. We'd settled on most of these details before Penny was born, and I found myself grateful, we had, since I couldn't imagine worrying about such trivial fucking things now. Despite our foresight, we still had no dining room table. It wouldn't arrive until after the new year, and my study consisted of a desk, empty shelves, and dozens of boxes waiting to be unpacked. My office in town was available if I needed a space to work, although I wouldn't be taking clients until Penny was a bit older.

Because, despite our intentions, Belle flat refused to hire any of the nannies we'd seen. The most I'd been able to convince her to do was speak with one of them about coming on in the future.

"I can't believe it."

I turned to look at Belle, who was staring at her phone. She raised her head, her eyes lit like the Christmas tree next to her, and grinned. "We got the deal with *Society*. They're going to publish our monthly curated looks."

She flew to me, arms wide and I turned into her. Her chin rested on my shoulder as she kissed my cheek.

"That's amazing, beautiful." I meant it. She'd taken her company, Bless, from an idea to a force in the fashion industry. But that wasn't what really mattered. I hadn't seen her this excited for weeks.

"Lola spoke with them. She's going to put things together and send them to me for approval. It will have to be a joint effort until I'm back from maternity leave," she rattled off all the details in a hushed voice while Penny continued to sleep in my arms.

"Your mum is famous," I whispered to Penny, and Belle smiled sheepishly, rolling her eyes.

"It's nothing." She shrugged and I could already sense the happiness fading from her. I wished I could find the place where it was seeping out and fix it.

"It's everything," I said quickly. "And you don't have to take maternity leave, beautiful."

She bristled and I rushed on before she could mistake what I was saying. "I'm here without any clients. We can always call Nora to come a few days a week, so we have an extra set of hands."

Belle bit her lower lip, a battle playing across her pale features. "Penny's too little for a nanny."

"Not a nanny. Just some help," I corrected her. I'd been thinking of how to bring this up for a while. "Penny could be with you while you worked and Nora could just hang out. Nora might even be an extra set of eyes for you."

"She's a little young to be our target demographic, but she did seem interested in Bless," Belle said thoughtfully. "Maybe just a couple afternoons a week."

"That makes sense," I said casually.

Belle took a deep breath, her eyes finding the floor, before she finally lifted them and whispered, "Am I a bad mum if I miss working?"

I shook my head, sighing, feeling as though a missing piece of an unfinished puzzle had finally appeared.

"How can you be sure?"

"If I told you I needed to meet a client in the village, what would you say?" I asked.

"I guess I'd just ask when and how long you'd be gone." Her eyebrows furrowed together. "But you aren't taking clients."

"That's not the point. It wouldn't be odd for me to ask, so you shouldn't feel guilty for working either," I pointed out.

"It's not like we need the money. I should be the one home with Penny," she continued.

"And you will be." I turned and kissed her forehead. "If anyone can be a brilliant business woman and a super mum, it's you."

"Are you sure?" The corners of her mouth twitching like she might actually smile.

"I'll always bet on you," I promised, meaning it with all my heart.

15

BELLE

"I think that's everything," I announced to Nora, wishing that I felt as confident as I sounded. Lola had insisted on driving the two hours from Silverstone to Sussex to celebrate the latest big milestone for Bless. I'd tried to talk her out of it, but only half-heartedly. The truth was that the idea of seeing a friend had me more excited than I'd felt since we'd left hospital with Penny. Naturally, Lola's visit coincided with the same day the new gardener was starting on, leaving Smith and I to our first real attempt to juggle having an infant and dealing with the outside world.

Nora poked her head over the changing bag. "Do you want me to check?"

I shook my head. I wasn't about to admit to her that I'd written out a checklist last night and memorized it. It was only her second day on with us, but I didn't want her thinking I was completely helpless. She was an extra pair of hands like Smith had said. She was just here to make life easier, not replace me. "I think we're ready."

She picked it up, not questioning me more, and swung it over her shoulder. "Do you want me to carry her down?"

I nodded, passing Penny to her. "I'm just going to grab my purse."

We were leaving with more than enough time to spare. Smith had pulled the Range Rover around to the front drive and warmed it up. The only thing left was to check my lipstick and drive into town. I couldn't deny that despite the happiness I felt, I dreaded today a little, too. It was the first time I was attempting to take the baby out socially. Yes, I would have Nora there, but I wanted things to go smoothly. If I thought I'd have to spend one more day trapped inside Thornham, wandering the halls like a prisoner, I might go mental.

I was most of the way to the front door when Mrs. Winters caught me. "Will you be taking dinner at the normal hour?"

I suspected that Mrs. Winters was horrified by Smith's and my lack of decorum. Given that we had no formal dining room, we often took dinner in the kitchen with whatever staff was around for the evening. Some nights we skipped an evening meal entirely. On more than one occasion, she'd cooked a whole meal only to discover we weren't hungry. We'd quickly learned that on those nights, we were expected to eat whether we wanted to or not. It was a lot less like having a housekeeper and more like having an overbearing governess.

"I suppose it would be better to ask Mr. Price. I don't know how long he'll be with Rowan."

Her mouth pinched into a grim line, revealing a mapwork

of wrinkles. "Customarily, the lady of the house makes these decisions."

I bit my tongue before I could tell her that I was about as far from a lady as she could imagine.

"I guess you'll have to settle for the gentleman of the house." I hoped she used that terminology with Smith. The only thing more suspect than calling me a lady was thinking of him as a gentleman.

Not that he'd been his usual self in that regard since Penny was born.

"And will Miss Welter be dining with you?"

I could tell from the way she asked that the idea of the nanny eating dinner with the family was even more scandalous than my disinterest in running the household like we were in a nineteenth century novel.

"For fuck's sake, I don't know," I exploded. Mrs. Winters grimaced slightly but maintained her composure. I suppose she now knew exactly how much of a lady I was. "I'm sorry. I don't want to be late, and the baby is in the car."

"Of course, I would never dream of keeping you from your child," she said in a clipped tone, but there was a current running through her words like a trickle of ice cold water.

I felt considerably less buoyant as I stepped out the front door, shrugging my Burberry trench coat over my shoulders. A loud whistle sliced through the air, followed by Smith's voice. "I'm not certain the village is prepared for you."

My husband's feet, clad in chestnut-leather hunting boots, crunched along the gravel pathway toward me, a smirk carved on his handsome face. Smith had acclimated to the country with enviable ease. His Barbour jacket fit him like he'd been born to this lifestyle, its waxed canvas shell a deep olive-green that brought out his eyes. He'd turned up his brown corduroy collar against the wind, which had swept his hair into a sexy mess. Today he'd skipped his razor, leaving a noticeable stubble along his strong jaw. My core tightened at the sight of him. That had been happening more and more of late.

It was the only thing that was happening. I'd lost track of all the reasons why.

"I'll see you this evening," I said, descending the stairs. "Where's Rowan?"

"Apparently, he doesn't need my opinion on how to run an estate," Smith said ruefully.

My mouth gaped. "He didn't?"

"In fairness, he's right. I don't think the month we spent with your mother actually counts as real experience." He bent to sweep a kiss over my lips, when he finally straightened up, his green eyes stormed. "I'm not certain I want you to leave, after all."

I licked my lower lip, searching for signs that he meant it. I'd managed to wriggle into a pre-pregnancy pair of black, leather pants and a white silk blouse that buttoned too low to be proper for a countryside luncheon. Smith caught the lapels of my cashmere coat and tugged them together.

"I don't think Mrs. Winters approves of me going out like this," I murmured to him. "Actually, I don't think she approves of me in general."

"Who cares, beautiful?" he muttered. "Although, I think I'd rather you stay home and work if you're going to wear something like this. It reminds me of sneaking peeks at your breasts when you worked for me."

"Sir," I said in mock horror. "If I'd known you were looking…"

"Oh, you knew," he growled. "Maybe when you come back, you could give me another peek at—"

"Sorry to interrupt," Nora's voice called, and we broke apart to find her head popping out of the Range Rover's back seat, a low cry filling the air behind her. "But she's not fond of her car seat."

"On my way!" I ducked under Smith's arm, throwing a kiss over my shoulder at him. It was the first time in weeks I felt like he meant his flirtations. He hadn't chosen each word carefully. He hadn't avoided touching me. I'd begun to worry that he didn't see me the same way after Penny was born. It's not like I could blame him for being tentative after that. Truthfully, I rarely found myself even thinking about things like sex these days. Why had I waited so long to bring Nora on? I already felt more like my old self.

That feeling fled from me as I climbed into the driver's seat to discover Penny was no longer fussy, but pissed.

"Sorry, darling," I called.

"I think I better stay back here," Nora said. "She'll calm down once we get going."

I hesitated for a moment. I should be the one back there, trying to calm her down. What if she just got more and more upset? But more than anything I wanted today to be as normal as possible. She'd calm down like Nora said and I'd have a moment of normal for the first time in weeks, I decided as I shifted into drive and started toward the village. It was time to get back to the real world.

16

SMITH

"Detective Longborn called," Humphrey informed me as I stepped into the mudroom. The first time I tracked mud into the foyer I'd learned the hard way that this was Mrs. Winters' house—I only happened to live here.

"What did he want?" I loosened the twin straps at the top of my boot, giving me enough room to yank it off. I left the pair of them on a berber rug by the back door. Shucking off my jacket, I ran a hand under the collar of my wool sweater to soothe the goddamn constant itching it caused.

"Apparently, there's been some development regarding the situation in the wine cellar," he said meaningfully.

"The bones?" I asked. I had barely thought about them in weeks. I'd been too distracted with everything else going on at Thornham to worry about someone else's tragedy.

"He'd like to meet with you."

I heaved a sigh. The trouble with living in the countryside was that people were constantly inventing drama out of sheer boredom. No wonder half the country's television programs were about little old ladies solving murders in idyllic country towns. "I'll phone him."

I'd only gotten a few steps inside the kitchen when Mrs. Winters confronted me, a long wooden spoon resting ominously in her palm. If Belle thought the old housekeeper—who doubled as our cook, per her own request—disliked her, she hated me and did little to hide it. Part of me wondered what she had against me. At first I'd thought it might have to do with being Scottish, but she'd been warm enough to Rowan, who took pride in his heritage to a concerning level. I suspected she simply disliked working in a less than traditional household.

"Mrs. Winters, how are you?" I asked, doing my best to be polite as my patience wore thin. I'd had very little sleep last night. Belle had taken to sleeping through Penny's cries until I shook her awake. At least, she was acting more like herself during the day.

"Well, that depends, Mr. Price," she said in a stern voice, and I braced myself, "on whether my services are actually needed in this house?"

I frowned. There was no way we could keep on top of all this space, especially with a newborn demanding most of our attention. "Of course. You're essential."

"Then, you don't like my cooking?" she demanded.

I blinked. "Your cooking is fine."

"Then what time would you like dinner served every night?" she asked through gritted teeth.

I'd guessed it was about something as simple as this. Belle and I weren't likely to start living a traditional country lifestyle anytime soon, not while her business was growing so swiftly or I was starting my own practice, but if we didn't make some changes, we were going to have a mutiny on our hands. Rowan wanted to be left to do his work in peace. Humphrey never seemed to have anything to do, given our lack of visitors. Half of me thought he only existed in the pockets of time in which we needed him. I never saw him save for when he appeared to deliver a message. And Mrs. Winters took our liberal schedule as a personal insult.

"Seven," I answered her. "I'll be certain Belle knows, and if we're caught at work, you can save us plates."

"Save you plates?" she echoed.

I adopted my best lawyer voice, the one I saved for dealing with particularly difficult clients. "I'm afraid it will take us some time to adjust from our lives in London to Thornham."

The stern angles of her face softened slightly.

"And the baby," I added, certain this would be the lynchpin to my argument. She couldn't possibly disagree with the struggles of new parents.

"Perhaps, if the missus was more focused on her babe, she wouldn't be running around looking for happiness."

"Belle prefers *Ms.*," I informed her, dropping all pretense of formality. "Belle is a wonderful mother."

"Of course, she is, Mr. Price," she said with a cold smile that chilled me to my bones. "But, word to the wise, a woman can be a wonderful mother and unhappy."

Her words were still ringing in my ears when I stepped into my study to phone Detective Longborn. Other than a few important documents regarding our purchase of Thornham, I hadn't gotten around to unpacking, so I was surprised to discover half the boxes there'd been the last time

I'd been in here. On my desk, Belle's elegant script was dashed across a notepad.

I took a few minutes while Nora was here to unpack a bit. Hope you don't mind.

I smiled, feeling vindicated in pushing for the nanny to finally start. There was no way I was going to admit it to Belle, but I'd been feeling restless myself. On one hand, I could lose myself for hours watching Penny sleep. The rest of the time, I found myself...bored. I'd been warned when we purchased this house that I'd need at least a skeleton staff to be certain things would run smoothly. I'd taken the advice, not wanting to worry about running a house and having a new baby. The trouble was that I was completely redundant now. Belle had Penny to look after, as well as Bless. Penny had Belle and Nora now. Rowan worried about the grounds. Mrs. Winters ran the household. And Humphrey took care of everything else. I was still stewing on this when Longborn answered his phone.

"Detective? Smith Price," I said in a clipped tone.

"Ah, Price. Thank you for returning my call."

"I assume there's been an update on the finding at Thornham." He'd told me he would call with any news. I hadn't expected there to be any.

"Perhaps I could come by and speak to you in person?" he suggested.

"If you like," I said slowly. It was never a good sign when the police wanted to chat, but that had been my experience in the city—where things actually happened. I reminded myself that this was just a symptom of living in the middle of the countryside.

"I'll stop by in a few days." I heard papers rustle on his desk.

"Should I be concerned?" I asked. I'd finally stopped dreaming of the pile of bones they'd found in my basement. I suspected they'd be making another appearance tonight.

Longhorn didn't respond immediately. His hesitation said more than our entire call. "It's likely nothing, but I'd rather tie this up."

"Of course." I hung up with him, my feet already carrying me to the lift. I rode it down to the quiet lower level. The swimming pool pump hummed in the background. If I turned that direction, I would find myself in it's muggy surroundings. Instead, I walked the opposite direction to the wine cellar and it's almost preternaturally cool space. It's why I'd chosen it for the wine cellar, but as I ran a finger over its stone walls, I found myself wondering what secrets these walls kept—and whether we'd unearth them.

BELLE

Lola squealed, jumping up from the table as soon as I entered The Briar Rose Inn holding Penny in my arms. The baby had only stopped crying when Nora unbuckled her from the seat and handed her to me with a sympathetic smile. I couldn't help being glad that she wasn't greeting my business partner with screams. Lola hugged me around the shoulder, peeking at Penny.

"She's gorgeous, just like her mama," Lola murmured, reaching to offer Penny a finger.

"She's a diva," I warned her.

"So she *is* just like you," Lola said with a laugh. "Come see your Aunt Lola." She scooped the baby up, turning her for further inspection. Penny responded by spitting up all over her fitted blazer. Lola winced but forced a bright smile. "This is why I'm childless."

"I'm so sorry." I turned to find Nora already digging in the baby bag for something to wipe up the mess. She finally found a burp cloth, and she passed it apologetically to Lola.

Lola passed the baby back to her, shaking her head, as she

dabbed at the spot. "It's nothing, and it's black, so you can't even notice."

"Her tummy was probably a bit upset from the car," Nora said. "She's not fond of the drive."

"Oh, I should have come to you!" Lola's eyes widened with a clear question: why hadn't I said anything?

I had to bite back a saucy response. Lola could have come to me, but I hadn't wanted her to. I'd been dying for an excuse to get out of Thornham. The problem was there wasn't much to do in the local village and given the wintery weather, I couldn't justify dragging an infant out to explore. Lola's visit was the perfect reason to go into town.

"It's no trouble," I said. "We didn't mind at all." I shot Nora a look that dared her to contradict me.

"I got us a table. I had to fight people off for it." Lola grinned mischievously as we joined her at the corner table. The Briar Rose was completely empty, which wasn't exactly a surprise given the time of day and the fact that it was the fanciest of restaurants—by the standards of the village of Briarshead. The bistro had clearly once been a house, but had been converted into a mix of pub and fine dining. It was too sophisticated to qualify as the former but not posh enough to be the latter. A wood stove was lit in the corner and abstract art decorated the walls. The tables and chairs were an eclectic mix of styles artfully chosen rather than merely crashing. A chalkboard listed the day's specials, which were also a combination of traditional English fare and French dishes.

"We probably would have had more options in London," I said, looking around.

"I wanted to see where you lived, and you don't need to drag Penny all the way to the city."

I bit my lip, forcing a smile. It was thoughtful of her. We'd only just settled into Thornham. Of course, we didn't need to go to London, so why did my heart ache at the idea?

"I think this little one needs to be changed," Nora announced. "Fingers crossed there's a spot in the loo."

"Oh, I didn't..." I stared at her. It hadn't even occurred to me that this might be a problem.

"I've changed plenty of babies on the floor." Nora cuddled her close. "It will be fine. Enjoy yourself."

"You should take your nanny's advice," Lola said as Nora disappeared down the hall with the baby. "Although, now that she's gone, I can tell you that you are a brave woman."

"Huh?" But before she could explain what she meant, a waiter arrived with two glasses of champagne.

"Oh! Good! Drink up! We're celebrating." Lola tapped hers to mine. "To Bless and dreams come true."

I repeated her words and took a sip, waiting for a moment to properly acknowledge the toast. "What did you mean? About me being brave?"

"Your nanny is smoking hot," she said seriously. "I don't think most women would want someone like that around."

I opened my mouth, searching for a response and finding none. I'd thought about this before Penny arrived. I'd even joked with Smith about it. I'd convinced myself it didn't matter, but now Lola was here pointing it out.

"I'm being a bitch, aren't I?" Lola said with a frown, lowering her champagne flute. "Ugh, Anders isn't here to call me on it. I'm sorry. That was a thoughtless thing to say. She's not any prettier than you and it's not like Smith would even notice another woman."

I swallowed the rest of my champagne in a single gulp. I

was delivered from more awkward apologies by the return of the waiter. He drew a small notepad out of his canvas apron pocket, blowing a strand of brown hair from his eyes.

"What do you suggest?" Lola said, her eyes scrolling across the options on the blackboard.

"Most people opt for the fish and chips," he informed us.

Something about the weary way he spoke sparked in me. "What's the best thing on the menu? We're celebrating."

"The guinea fowl," he said without hesitation.

"You sure?"

"I cooked it myself." He gave a crooked grin. "I'm afraid I'm pulling triple duty most weekdays."

"You're the cook?" Lola looked delighted by this news.

"And the owner, which sounds a lot more glamorous than it is," he admitted.

I couldn't help being surprised. He couldn't be much older than us. I guessed there was a story about how he'd wound up here with a restaurant, but I didn't want to pry.

"What are you celebrating?" He dropped into Nora's chair.

"What aren't we celebrating?" Lola asked. "Let's see her new baby and our business getting a column in the U.K.'s leading high fashion magazine...oh, and I guess, your new house."

"And you came to Sussex for that?" he said with a laugh.

"Her new house is here," Lola explained.

"Really? Welcome to town. Where did you move?"

"Thornham Park," I said.

He flinched. I cocked my head, checking to see if Lola caught it, too. From the quizzical look, she was giving him, she had.

"Sorry," he said quickly. "You spend enough time around these parts and you hear plenty about Thornham."

"All good, I hope," I said dryly. Considering we'd found skeletons during our remodel, I knew better than to expect that. I could only imagine what a small village like Briarshead whispered about a house as old as mine. Superstition and gossip. Still, I couldn't shake the way he'd reacted when I'd told him I lived there. A pit formed in my stomach, my hunger vanishing.

"What kind of things?" Lola pressed, interested in the detached way of someone who didn't have to return to sleep there. I wanted to tell them to drop it, but I found myself curious.

"The usual ghost stories." He shrugged. "The place is hundreds of years old. It's all nonsense." He looked at me with a soft smile. "The champagne is on me."

"Oh, I couldn't—"

"Consider it a housewarming present..."

"Belle," I told him, holding out a hand.

To my surprise, he didn't shake it, he kissed it. I flushed as he smiled up at me. I couldn't remember the last time a man had been so forward with me. Then again, I'd been hugely pregnant for months, and I usually had a protective alpha male at my side.

"Enchantée, Belle. I'm Tomas," he told me.

Before I could be too embarrassed, he turned and took Lola's hand. She giggled as she introduced herself. Before he could continue his seduction attempts, Nora appeared holding a shrieking baby. I stood so quickly, my chair clattered to the floor. Guilt washed over me. I'd nearly forgotten she was off with Nora. What kind of mother was I? Letting a strange French man kiss my hand while my baby was off with her nanny?

"What's wrong?" I switched into anxious mum mode instantly.

"I'm so sorry." Nora looked genuinely horrified as she bounced from foot to foot. "But there's no nappies in the bag."

"What? I packed them!" I swiped the bag from her, rifling through it anxiously, each second growing more aware of Lola and Tomas's eyes on me as Penny screamed.

There were none. I'd made a list. I'd laid awake planning, worried I would screw something up—and I had. How had I forgotten something as basic as nappies?

"There's a shop on the corner," Tomas said kindly.

"I'll go grab them," Nora said. She moved to pass Penny to me and I took her, rocking swiftly in a desperate attempt to calm her. But my daughter only seemed more upset to be with me. Her howling cries splintered the last remnants of my self-control and I dissolved into tears as Nora disappeared to find nappies.

"Sorry," I croaked, shushing Penny to no effect.

"Forget the guinea fowl," Tomas said. "I'll be right back."

As soon as he was gone, I turned and for one moment, Lola looked so much like her sister that I blurted out a confession, "She doesn't like me."

"Oh, Belle." Lola stood, moving closer to me and stroking my arm. "That's not true. She's just uncomfortable."

"Because of me," I sobbed. "I can't even pack a changing bag properly."

"Let me," Lola said, gently taking Penny from her arms. She was bright red from screaming, and being passed off only resulted in her skin deepening to purple as she howled louder. "See? She hates me, too!"

I forced myself to smile, even though the joke did nothing to soothe me. I couldn't believe that I'd let my business partner see me this unglued. As far as I knew, Lola had no interest in kids. I'd rarely even seen her around her niece and nephew. Now, thanks to me, she was cajoling a pissed off newborn instead of sipping champagne.

"Here. This will help," Tomas announced, placing a plate with a large, four-tiered slice of chocolate cake on the table. He waved me to the chair, passing me a cloth napkin. "Sit. Chocolate fixes everything."

I dropped into the chair, dabbing my eyes with the napkin. With both their eyes on me, I picked up a fork and took a small bite before managing a brittle smile. I was supposed to be the caregiver here. I was the mum, but everyone was busy taking care of me while my baby cried.

Because I couldn't calm her down.

Because I wasn't meant to be a mother.

That was why I'd had the miscarriage. That's why it had taken me a year to get pregnant again. It was why Smith hovered so much in the background when I had Penny. He could sense it. I'd felt his feelings toward me change since I gave birth. He could see right through me to the hollow, rotten core that was never meant to care for a child.

"Got them," Nora called brightly, coming back into the restaurant. Two more diners entered behind her, looking startled at the scene they'd stumbled upon.

I stood and grabbed Penny, holding out my hand for the shop bag. "I've got it."

"Do you want help?" Nora asked as she passed it to me.

"No, can you take my card out and pay? I don't want to disturb everyone else's lunch." I managed to say this evenly even as my heart beat so fast I thought I was going to crack open.

Carrying Penny to the bathroom, I discovered that Nora had been right earlier. There was nowhere to change the baby but the floor. Sinking down gracelessly, and realizing that my days of leather pants were long over, I spread the changing pad on the floor, and began changing her. Her nappy was so full that I started to cry again with her. I'd done this to her. As soon as I'd cleaned her up, she calmed down, yawning widely, exhausted from what I'd put her through. Snapping up her romper, I cradled her close to my shoulder as I repacked the bag, shoving the nappies inside it along with the dirty one.

Standing, I caught a glimpse of myself in the mirror over the sink. I didn't recognize the woman staring back at me. I needed a haircut. Despite doing my make-up earlier, bluish circles ringed my eyes—eyes so bloodshot that they nearly matched my lipstick. I looked like I'd walked out of a horror movie. The sleepy bundle at my shoulder nuzzled against me, and the stranger in the mirror cringed.

Except it wasn't a stranger reflected there. It was me, and for the first time, I saw the truth as I held my little girl:

I wasn't struggling. I wasn't adjusting. I simply *wasn't*.

Wasn't meant to be a mother, wasn't happy, wasn't ready.

And, in that moment, I wished Penny had never been born.

18

SMITH

I spent the afternoon performing comforting rituals. Belle had unpacked a few boxes worth of books and begun to set up my desk, but there was still plenty to do. The menial tasks kept my hands occupied, but they weren't enough to keep me from thinking about Longborn's call. When we made the grisly discovery in the wine cellar I told myself this was natural for a house of this age. Longborn himself had said it. Now, it seemed there was more to the story. I went about the room, absentmindedly alphabetizing a series of law journals until the last volume was in place.

In truth, the whole process was rather pointless. We didn't need me to go back to taking clients. Between the London real estate I'd divested after marrying Belle, which included my holdings in Velvet, a private club and my family home, neither I nor my wife needed to work another day in our lives. That was easier said than done. I wasn't about to tell Belle to give up her company. But, if I was being honest, starting a law firm in Briarshead was more about the appearance of legitimacy then actually wanting to practice law. I'd expected Alexander to put up more of a fight when I told him we were leaving London. Perhaps, I thought too highly of the help I'd given him tracking Clara down a few months ago. Or, and this was much more likely, I'd underestimated his capacity for sympathy. Why would he deny me the decision to protect my wife and child? It was the motivation that drove him entirely. Naturally, he understood my position. But having his blessing meant I no longer needed a professional cover. That left me at an impasse.

Still, I couldn't help thinking I might be able to do some good. We didn't need the money, but maybe that was the missing piece. I took a seat behind my desk and stared at it. I'd studied law because Hammond wanted me to study law, because my father had been in law. I'd been another weapon in Hammond's arsenal, used to cover up the tracks of vice and criminal activity he needed to hide. I didn't exactly have a passion for the law, exactly, but I was very, very good at what I did.

It's why Hammond had walked for years free despite his crimes. I couldn't quite forgive myself all the wrong I had done on his behalf as his personal legal counsel. Perhaps, I could ease some of my guilt, though. I could offer my services *pro bono* to people in the village who couldn't afford legal representation. I could represent them to the town council or help them with custody or divorces or other small claims. I might actually be able to turn the sordid skills of my past into something valuable.

Or, I could stay home and fuck my wife.

I couldn't help feeling my ideal life lay somewhere in between the two.

Not that Belle had shown any interest in me since Penny's

arrival. We'd been given strict orders by the doctor to wait at least six weeks before resuming sexual activity. One had to presume that the doctor had meant boring vanilla sex, and not the intimacy which we craved from one another. Or that we used to want.

I still wanted her, but maybe she had forgotten. Penny had only hit six weeks a few days ago. Belle was up with her every night and tired during the day. We'd only just brought Nora on to help. And Belle had said things—cruel things—about herself during that time. Maybe she was just waiting for me to initiate and prove I still desired her.

My balls ached as I considered how I might go about proving it, and I adjusted them in my trousers.

As much as I wanted my wife *in every way*, as much as I'd hungered to take her *every day*, this was new territory to me. When I first met Belle, she talked a big game about *not* sleeping with me. I played along with it, assuming the role of her boss. Back then, sex had been inevitable between us. In those days, tension lingered in the air like static before a thunderstorm. She'd wanted it all the time. I'd given it to her whenever possible. It was an understanding. Now? There was nothing. No sign or indication of interest on her part. I reasoned with myself that she was tired and still adjusting to being a mother, but that left me wondering what would happen if I walked into our bedroom, picked her up, and fucked her against the wall until she remembered who she belonged to.

I wanted to every time I saw her. In the morning, when I caught glimpses of her stepping into the shower. At night, when she slipped off her robe and slid between the sheets. Nothing had changed in that regard. Except that I seemed to want her even more. I even found myself considering another baby, ready to see her round with the life I'd given her again.

But like my desires for intimacy, I kept these thoughts to myself almost instinctively. I knew somehow that bringing up another baby or future children would make her cry. I couldn't even allow myself to wonder if bringing up sex would do the same.

Because the truth was that I was more in love with my wife than ever before. But for the first time since we met, I wasn't sure she would say the same about me.

My mobile vibrated, its ringtone muffled by my leather desk pad. I reached for it, grateful for the distraction from the depressing thoughts intruding on my afternoon. I frowned when I saw Georgia's number flashing on the screen. She never called unless something was wrong. Considering the last time I had seen her, I'd asked her to look into Thornham's history, I braced myself as I answered. "Hello?"

"Yes, I'd like to speak to Lord Price. Is he available or is he out hunting or planning this evening's round of charades in the salon?" she responded dryly.

"Have you ever been to the country?" I asked, sinking into my desk chair, and smiling despite myself. "Or have you just seen period dramas on television?"

There was an unladylike snort on the other end. "I don't have time to go to the country, but yes I have been before."

I had a hard time picturing Georgia amongst the genteel country circle, politely gossiping with the ladies after dinner and riding out on horseback for the morning hunt on weekends. It wasn't her style. It wasn't mine either. All the more reason, I was going to have to find something to do with myself. From all indications, that was exactly what people did in the country. At least, visiting aristocrats and billionaires. Thornham was so far removed from the village that I didn't exactly have a great sense of what day-to-day life was like amongst its small population. But from what I'd seen of estate life, Georgia wasn't far off in her assumptions. "Did you need something?"

"I see that you've got the tuck-up part of living on an estate down" she answered. "I was calling with an update for you, but if you're too busy doing whatever it is you do out there, you can call me back later."

"Out with it," I said, trying not to sound too eager. The truth was that except for when I read through the *London Times* over my morning coffee, I hadn't kept up with anything going on in the city. With Belle and the baby gone for the day, I didn't know what to do with my time. An update from Georgia would at least distract me until they returned home.

"Fine. There's a sealed report about your house with the local police department."

"A sealed report?" I repeated. "What does it say?"

"How would I know? It's *sealed*," she said slowly, so I could keep up.

That was the thing about Georgia—she would help you out, but she'd make you work for it. "Sorry. I was under the impression you worked for the King of Great Britain."

"Whatever is in that file hasn't been digitized," she said. "I'd have to come and request it in person, or at least that's what the detective that answered told me."

"Longborn?"

"Something like that."

Everything fell into place. I'd been concerned about what Longborn was coming to tell me, but it hadn't occurred to me that he might find people digging into the history of the house suspicious. Georgia had probably triggered small-town paranoia, the kind that kept ghost stories alive, and now I would be receiving a personal visit from the officer to ensure everything was on the up and up.

"He called me this morning." I pinched the bridge of my nose, feeling a headache coming on. "I'd actually thought there might be something to worry about when he said he needed to speak with me. He probably just wants to know who the pushy bitch requesting old files is."

"Remind me not to do you any more favors," Georgia said, her tone flat.

"I'll request the file." I couldn't imagine what I'd owe her if she actually came down here and got the report in person. Possibly my second born.

"Something tells me he won't like that," Georgia said thoughtfully.

"Why would he care about an old file?" I asked.

"I don't know. But I wasn't a *pushy bitch* with him," she said. I could almost picture her air quoting me. "I tried everything to get him to send me that file. I was sugar-sweet, Price, and he wouldn't budge."

"You know how things are in a village," I said to her. "They have to abide by their red tape or they have nothing to do."

"Well, if you find out more, I want to know," Georgia said. "I want to know what's hiding in your basement."

"Nothing's hiding in my basement," I snapped. At the same moment the door down the hall slammed shut, startling me. I checked my Omega and frowned. Either Mrs. Winters was upset about something and slamming doors, or Belle's lunch date had been cut short. For once, I'd rather deal with an irritated housekeeper than discover something had gone wrong for my wife's trip out. "I need to go. It sounds like a dead end, anyway."

"I'll keep looking into it."

I opened my mouth to tell her not to bother, but she'd already hung up. It was a waste of Georgia's time to keep looking into this, especially if it was as simple as getting a file from Longborn. I wanted to know more about the skeletons they found of my property, but I couldn't deny that all evidence pointed to a rational explanation for their presence. We'd probably simply disturbed an old grave, excavating to add to the casks. Sometimes, I wondered if my time in London had warped my perception of the world. Had I begun to see evil doing when there was only coincidence? I needed to focus on here and now, starting with checking on my wife. The hallway was so eerily quiet, I'd begun to think I'd imagined it. I poked my head into the guest rooms and the nursery, finding both empty. As I walked toward my room, the door opened and Nora ducked out. She took two steps in my direction before looking up. When she did she froze in her tracks, letting out a tiny yelp.

"I'm sorry to scare you," I said. I looked over her shoulder at the bedroom door she'd closed behind her. "I thought I heard someone come in."

"Lunch ended a little more quickly than expected," Nora said, choosing her words carefully. I recognized a lawyer's trick when I heard one. She was telling the truth but leaving out the important bits. Her eyes skirted away from me as she spoke, and I wondered what had made her so nervous. Before I could ask her, the bedroom door opened again, revealing a harassed-looking Belle, bouncing the baby wearily. When she saw me, she sighed.

That was new. I told myself it meant nothing, but even something as simple as finding me at our bedroom door seemed to annoy her.

"Can one of you take her? I need to lie down."

I stepped forward, arms open and accepted Penny. "Are you feeling alright?"

My question was cut off by the bedroom door closing. I turned to Nora, hoping for answers, but she only smiled. "I can take her to the nursery if you like. I still have a few more hours scheduled here."

"Why don't you check in with Mrs. Winters?" I suggested. "She usually does Penny's laundry in the morning. It might be nice if Belle woke up to everything done."

"I can do that." She nodded enthusiastically, and I thought I caught a bit of relief on her face as she headed toward the spiral staircase that led to the lower levels.

What was that about? Had the baby been more than a handful? Something brought them home early. Now Belle was locked in our bedroom and the new nanny was avoiding eye contact. I hoped I was simply reading into things. I carried Penny back to my study. Whatever had been wrong earlier during their trip, she seemed content to sleep in my arms now. I half heartedly organized the papers on my desk with one free hand, mostly focused on enjoying the feeling of my daughter nuzzled against my chest. I sorted a stack to file and reached to open a desk drawer. I kept my father's gun in the top drawer, so I opted for the lower one. When I opened it, I froze, spying the edge of a familiar picture frame.

When I decided to close my London office, I placed most of its furnishings and files into storage. There'd been no where to put them in our Holland Park home, so this was the first time in nearly six months that I'd sat at this desk. But even six months ago, the framed photograph of my late wife had been packed away in some dusty corner box in my office. I hadn't looked at a picture of Margot since the moment I realized I was in love with Belle. I'd let Margot go then, consigning her to memories I rarely called to mind. Still, she was there in the back of my mind, intruding on my thoughts at the worst times. I'd failed her. Or she had failed me. The only thing I was certain enough about was that our marriage had been a disaster. More than that, it had been another of Hammond's devious attempts to control me. He'd alluded to being behind the car accident that took her life, although he never had a chance to tell me why. Someone had murdered him before he came clean. I could have asked the last time I saw him alive—the time at which he admitted manipulating me into marrying her. I'd been too furious at that revelation to seek answers. Not because I hadn't suspected it to be the truth, but because, despite everything, it had shown me how foolish I had been.

Belle had been another of his manipulations, but that had backfired. She had shown me what love truly was and made me willing to fight for ours.

And, it seemed, while she had been unpacking my things, she'd come across this photograph of Margot and placed it here. I couldn't guess why. Maybe that was a passive way to confront me about finding it amongst my possessions. But I'd rather she had yelled at me, so I could apologize and throw the thing rather than find it shoved in a drawer. Or maybe, and somehow this was worse, she thought I wanted it here and had quietly seen to my wishes. If she'd been truly angry, she would have taken the gun she must have found when she was sorting through my things and hunted me down.

I leaned down, cradling Penny against me carefully so that I wouldn't wake her as I took the frame out of the drawer. Laying it on the desk, I looked around and realized there was no rubbish bin for me to toss it in.

There was a light knock on the door and I called out, "Come in."

"I'm sorry to disturb you." Nora shuffled into the room, her arms empty. Mrs. Winters must not have done the washing yet. "I'd like to talk to you about something."

I stood and circled around my desk. "Take her, so we can find somewhere to sit."

Nora accepted Penny with ease. She looked like a natural holding the baby. Belle had chosen correctly, despite her concerns about Nora's age.

I dug out a chair from under a few boxes of books and moved it across from my desk. "Have a seat."

I hesitated, wondering if I should take the baby back, but Nora continued to hold her, sinking in the chair, her teeth chewing on her lower lip. I returned to my chair, a pit opening in my stomach. What could have made her nervous this early into her position with us.

Nora's eyes were on my desk, and too late, I realized she was staring at the photograph of Margot.

"She's pretty," Nora said conversationally. "Your sister?"

Margot had been beautiful. Hammond always made sure the women he dangled over my cage were tempting enough to distract me. But everything about Margot had been false. Beneath her beauty, there had been a void. She'd filled it with champagne and drugs and whatever man caught her eye. I'd done the same. We'd lived that life together, and I told myself that was what love was. I was young and stupid enough to believe it. She was beautiful and wild and everything a stupid, reckless boy could want.

"Not exactly," I said, leaving it at that. I was having a hard enough time explaining to myself why there was a picture of my dead wife in my office. I didn't really want to get into it with the nanny. "What do you need to talk to me about?"

"I want to tell you that I'm enjoying Penny and being here," she began. I recognized a preface when I heard one. I'd made enough arguments in front of the courts to know one when someone was about to deliver a carefully crafted speech. Whatever was weighing on Nora, she had some time to think about it. But she'd only been here a few days. What had she seen that I hadn't? She took a deep breath, before continuing, "I'm concerned about your wife."

"Belle?" I said.

"Unless you have another one," she said with a nervous laugh.

I wondered then if she guessed who the woman in the photo really was, and if so what she thought of me: a married man with a new baby looking at pictures of his dead wife. I was beginning to feel out of sorts.

When I didn't respond, she cleared her throat before pressing forward, "I'm sure you've noticed that Belle's been sad lately."

She chose the word carefully. I knew by how much emphasis she placed on it.

"The doctor said to expect this," I told her, wanting to assuage her fears. "Hormonal shifts and whatnot."

"Yes, I'm sure it can be." She looked at Penny, who was still sleeping in her arms. "But I'm not sure it's that simple."

"Did something happen today?" I asked, thinking of how they came home early with Belle already needing a nap.

"I don't want to tell tales," she said with hesitation. "It's not really my place."

"My wife and I have no secrets. If she hasn't told me what happened, it's only because she's resting. You should never be concerned to tell me anything, particularly if it involves our daughter. I want to be as involved as I can be."

"In that case," she said slowly, "It was really silly. She forgot the nappies in the changing bag. I found a stack just now in the nursery. Not exactly a big deal."

"But it might be if you needed one," I said, guessing where the story went.

Nora nodded, shifting a little as Penny stirred. "Belle had every right to be frustrated, but..."

"Did something else happen?" I asked, worry beginning to take hold.

"She couldn't stop crying. We got the nappies and she went to change her. She wouldn't let me help. When she came back, she said we had to leave. She wouldn't talk at all on the way home."

I sat silently for a moment, contemplating what she said. I wasn't surprised to hear my wife had been crying. I'd witnessed plenty of that myself. "I'll speak with her about it."

"I don't want her to be angry with me," Nora said.

"I won't tell her you told me," I said with a reassuring smile. "I'll let her tell me herself."

"I just thought — it's not really my place – but maybe she should speak to a doctor," she said, adding quickly, "I'm sorry. That was too forward of me."

"You have my wife's best interest at heart," I said gruffly. "Your honesty is always welcome when it comes to keeping my family safe."

This seemed to appease her, and her rigid shoulders relaxed a little. I'd eased the burden she carried by adding it to my own shoulders— where it belonged.

"I'm going to take this little one into the nursery," Nora said, "and give you a little quiet time."

I didn't miss the suggestion in her voice. I was being sent to check on Belle. I was grateful Nora was here so that I could have a moment alone with my wife. As much as we both loved Penny, we'd barely had a moment together since she'd been born. It was all the more reason to have Nora around. And I appreciated that she'd come to speak with me, even if it wasn't news I wanted to hear.

It was a wake-up call—a reminder that I was too close to the situation. I'd expected things to get better, without really knowing if they would. I stood, picking up Margot's photograph and shoved it in an empty box by my desk. I would get rid of that later. Right now, I needed to check on my wife. I strode out of the office and down the hall to her bedroom. Cracking the door carefully, I peeked inside. The silk curtains we'd closed at night were drawn open, and afternoon light seeped through the window, haloing her body. I wandered over, worried I would disturb her. As much as I wanted a moment alone with her, she hadn't been sleeping well. Maybe she really just needed a nap. I climbed quietly into bed behind her, doing my best not to rouse her and molded by body against hers. I breathed in the light orange blossom scent perfuming her neck. She'd once told me she slept better when I was near her. So, maybe we hadn't had sex for a while, but holding her felt damn near as good.

A soft tremble rose in her chest, and I stilled. It took a moment before I processed what I was hearing. I thought Belle's breathing was soft snores, but, now that she was in my arms, I realized, with horror, that she was crying again.

"Beautiful?" I said gently.

A sob racked her. I nudged her carefully, urging her to roll over to face me. When she did, her eyes were rigged with the black remnants of her makeup. This had to end. I couldn't allow her to suffer like this.

"You're going to the doctor," I said, making the decision for her.

"But—"

"It's not an option, beautiful," I cut her off, pulling her closer to me. She didn't protest again. I had no idea if I was doing the right thing, but I would stay by her until she found her way out of the dark.

19

BELLE

The clinic in the village was a far cry from the office where I was seen during my pregnancy. I'd agreed to Smith's request to see a doctor, but we both felt driving all the way to London meant either packing Penny up and hoping for the best, or making me more stressed out about leaving her behind for the better part of the day. I'd been the one to finally decide on the local doctor. I'd committed to moving to Briarshead. Did I really want to go to London every time I had a cold?

Still, it felt odd being here now. The clinic was clean, sterilized to the point of something more like obsession than germ warfare. Nora followed behind me, Penny in her arms, as I stopped to wait for the only other patient here to move away from the check-in desk. It was an older woman, and I could tell by the laughter coming from the nurse that she likely wasn't here for more than a social call. I tapped my foot, feeling impatient. This was the last place I wanted to be, and now I had to wait.

I couldn't argue with Smith's concern. I sensed it myself. I simply found myself disinterested in doing anything about it. What could a doctor do? A doctor couldn't fix my brain and make me a competent mother. A doctor couldn't make certain I'd packed the nappies. I had Nora for that now.

She was a bit like having a shadow, to be honest. She moved into Thornham almost immediately after we asked her, on the understanding that it would be a short-term situation. She still planned to attend school later in the spring. But I got the impression that she felt guilty after what I'd deemed the chocolate cake incident. I still hadn't told Smith about what happened. I couldn't imagine what he would think of me for breaking down and sobbing into a dessert in front of my business partner and a total stranger, especially over something as stupid as forgetting to put nappies in the changing bag. I'd managed to reason with myself since the disastrous luncheon, realizing that no harm had been done. There had been a shop. We had found nappies. Lola hadn't quit Bless and, as far as I knew, Tomas would welcome me back in his restaurant any time. That meant, the only person I was being hard on was myself.

I just had to be a better mother. End of story.

"Excuse me," I interrupted as another laugh rose between the two. "I have an appointment."

"Bless me, I'm sorry!" The stub of a woman in front of me waived an apology as she turned around. "I didn't even hear you come in. I'll catch up with you later, Marjorie."

"Name?" The woman behind the desk—Marjorie, it seemed—asked, looking less apologetic then her friend. I doubted there were a lot of appointments on the books today, but I answered her all the same.

"Belle Stuart. I mean, Price," I said quickly, feeling embarrassed to have given my family name instead of my married name.

"I have you right here Mrs. Price," she said, passing the clipboard. "I just need you to sign a few documents for the NHS."

"*Ms. Price* will do," I told her, taking the clipboard and shuffling over to the seat next to Nora. Penny had stayed asleep for the entire ride into the village, already making this trip more successful than our last attempt at an outing. I suspected it had something to do with the presence of her nanny. Penny always seemed calm around Nora. I was grateful.

I was also a little jealous.

I signed the paperwork, wondering how Nora managed to make it all look so easy. Maybe the fact that she wasn't responsible for the entire growth, safety, and development of her charge made it easier to just relax and take care of her. I wouldn't know.

Lately, I found myself checking Penny obsessively to make certain she was breathing when she was quiet. I supposed I'd grown so accustomed to her screaming that I didn't know what to do with her when she wasn't crying.

I finished the forms and returned them to Marjorie. She peered at them with hawk-like eyes, sweeping across the lines until she reached the final page. "Seems to be in order. Will the doctor be seeing the baby as well?"

"I don't know," I said, truthfully. "She's six weeks old."

"And has she been seen for her six week check?"

I shook my head, remembering only now that I'd meant to put one on the books.

"I'm sure the doctor will want to see her then. She's due for her checkup," Marjorie said.

Heat pricked my eyes, and I blinked stubbornly against the tears. "I forgot. I'm sorry."

"It's a lot for a first-time mum," Marjorie said, warming up as she looked me over. "She would've let you know if something was wrong, dear."

Not that I would have been able to decipher that, I thought glumly.

"Why don't you go back and talk with Dr. Stanton alone first?" Marjorie suggested. "The baby can join you after."

"Thank you," I said, not trusting myself to say anything more.

Marjorie probably thought I was an idiot. I couldn't blame her. I'd proven over and over again I was. I took a chair inside the small exam room and waited for the doctor. While I did, I read a poster, describing the important milestones I needed to be watching for where Penny's growth was concerned. I hadn't even been thinking about things like that. Tummy time? Was I supposed to be doing that? I'd seen Clara doing that with Elizabeth and Wills, but it never occurred to me that it was a mandatory activity. Apparently, there were a lot of things I didn't know I should be doing. By the time the door to the exam room opened, I had dissolved into tears. I looked up, eyes brimming, and swallowed hard.

Dr. Stanton blinked once, but that was the only sign of surprise he showed about finding me in this state. "Well, I see you just had a baby." He said it in a conversational way as he read my chart, but I suspected the comment had more to do with finding me sobbing on his exam table. "And you have postpartum depression, it seems."

"I know it's normal." I swiped at my eyes, regurgitating all of the information my obstetrician in London told me following Penny's birth. "It's only been six weeks. I know things will adjust."

Dr. Stanton lowered my file and studied me for a moment, his brown eyes crinkling under bushy white eyebrows. "Sounds like you have it all figured out."

I nodded.

"There's not going to be a test," he said gently. "You can be honest with me, Ms. Price."

"It's just more than I expected," I said, managing to keep my voice from cracking. "The transition, I mean. The sleep. The crying."

"Your crying or the baby's crying?" he asked.

"Both," I said without thinking.

"You are absolutely correct that there is a period of transition for most mothers. How they respond to the hormonal changes is different for every woman. The severity of your depression doesn't reflect on your abilities as a mother.

"I have no reason to be depressed," I confessed. I had this argument with myself in the mirror this morning. "I'm sure if I give it time—"

"Let me be clear," he cut me off. "There is nothing wrong with having postpartum depression. Often, a woman feels it makes them a bad mother if they admit it. Over the last 40 years, I've heard women tell me all sorts of things that they thought following the birth of their baby. Some of them said they thought they were going crazy. Some of them were surprised they didn't like being a mother more. Some of them felt like their life was spiraling out of control. It affects everyone differently. But there's a lot of things we can do to help you feel better."

I opened my mouth to protest, but found all of my arguments draining from me. Why had I come here if I was just going to argue with him? To make Smith happy? I'd gotten myself here. Why couldn't that be enough? When I finally found my words again, they surprised even me. "Why don't I want to be happy?"

"You do. It just feels impossible, so you try not to think about it," he said in a soft voice. "And when you try not to think about it, you can't find the energy to do anything about it, and then you just get used to it and you wonder if it's always been like this. Does anything I say feel familiar?"

I nodded. It wasn't exactly how I felt, but it was bloody close. "I just thought this was what it felt like to be a mum."

"I don't want to alarm you, but that's not a natural reaction," he said. "I think that there are a couple of things we can do to help you get through this. First of all, I'd like you to take a little quiet time for yourself every day. Walk around the village."

"We live in the country. We just bought Thornham."

His head tilted ever so subtly, and I found myself thinking about Tomas's reaction to me telling him the same thing. Maybe everyone in town knew Thornham. Maybe they gossiped about the rich Londoners who lived there. I could only imagine what people said about us. I could only imagine how much worse it would be when they found out that I was practically in the loony bin.

"Thornham has lovely grounds," he continued casually, making me wonder if I'd imagined it entirely. "Take a walk down to the pond."

"I didn't even know there was a pond. You must know Thornham better than I do," I said, doing my best to have a normal social interaction. He thought I could solve this all by taking a walk. He had more faith than I did.

"I recall when the Thorns still lived on the property, but that was decades ago," he said. "It must've been some work to get the house into shape."

"We barely finished before the baby came," I admitted.

"It sounds like you've had a stressful year," he said. "A new baby, a new house—it would be enough to make anyone anxious. That's why I would also like to prescribe antidepressants to you."

I fought the urge to tell him no. Instead, I opted for voicing a more reasonable concern. "Is it safe for me to take them? I'm still nursing."

"I think you would do better to ask if it is safe for the baby for you *not* to take them."

I couldn't argue with that. Instead, I swallowed again, hoping not to burst into tears in front of the doctor a second time.

"How are you sleeping?"

"How am I supposed to be sleeping?" I said dryly. I might not have been prepared for all the changes my life would encounter when I had Penny, but I'd known I would be getting less sleep.

"It seems you have help, but it's always difficult to rest with an infant in the house," he said, obviously referring to Nora. "And is your husband..."

"He's very helpful," I said swiftly. In truth, Smith deserved more credit than I did. He certainly tried harder.

"I'd like to prescribe a sleeping tablet as well," he said.

"You should only take it when you feel like you need to get very well rested or to catch up on sleep. Times when the baby is with her nanny or her father perhaps."

I wanted to argue with him about that. A sleeping pill sounded even worse than antidepressants, but the thought of actually getting rest was too tempting.

"Now, am I going to meet this little one?" he asked.

I squared my shoulders before nodding. I'd had my moment alone. The doctor was going to give me things to fix me. There was no reason I should dread Nora bringing the baby in now. Still, when Dr. Stanton stuck his head out and called for Marjorie to send them in, I had the strangest urge to run. But the moment that Nora appeared with Penny, the feeling evaporated. Maybe I didn't have everything figured out yet, but seeing my daughter sent warmth spreading through my chest. My bliss was short-lived as the doctor began his examination, which resulted in Penny screaming her head off in indignation.

I felt terrible, but I couldn't help giggling at how upset she got when he weighed her. My good humor vanished when he frowned. "Her weight is a little less than we would like to see at this stage. I'm going to give you a few recommendations for some herbs that will help you increase your milk supply, and I'd like you to bring her back in two weeks for another weight check."

Despite Dr. Stanton's continued assurances that there was nothing to worry about, I left the clinic clutching orders for multiple things from the pharmacy with a newfound guilt over Penny's lack of weight gain. If I'd been more with it, I would have noticed. I tried to tell myself that Smith hadn't noticed and neither had Nora. We'd no reason to suspect anything was wrong until the doctor told us, but I kept thinking of Marjorie's words. If something was wrong she would have let us know. Had she been trying to? Had the screaming and crying and night waking been her attempts? Had I been too busy feeling sorry for myself to realize that my baby was hungry?

We bundled Penny into her pram outside the clinic, opting to walk a few blocks down to the pharmacy in the village.

A few eyes followed us as we entered. I couldn't help thinking that the other patrons were whispering about us. They probably suspected I was the new owner of Thornham. A town as small as Briarshead needed all the gossip it could get. Then, I wondered with horror if Tomas had told everyone about my disastrous lunch date at his restaurant. But for some reason, I was sure he hadn't. He didn't seem like the type to engage in small-minded gossip. I paused at the counter and passed Dr. Stanton's orders to the pharmacist there. She scanned them and nodded. "Give me a few minutes."

"Do you have a loo?" I asked her.

She tipped her head towards the door near the back. In London, it would've been impossible to find a public restroom. I supposed one of the perks of living in a tiny village was that since everyone knew who you were, no one could refuse you the toilet.

I walked over to Nora, peeking in to find Penny sleeping in her pram. "I'm going to use the loo. Are you alright?"

"We're fine. She's sleeping like an angel." She flashed me a bright smile, and I felt another prick of jealousy.

As I made my way to the loo, I found myself hoping that Dr. Stanton was right. I would take walks and medicine and do anything if it meant being able to look at Penny and not see my own failures. I took my time, relishing the few minutes of quiet. The pharmacy was small enough that I was certain I would hear Penny if she woke up. When I finally ducked out, the pharmacist called over. "I have them for you here."

I paid for the prescriptions and a tin of tea with the herbs he'd recommended. Then I found Nora looking at the menial selection of paperback romances the shop stocked at the counter. She put *Seducing the Sultan* back on the shelf, grinning sheepishly. "Got everything?"

I clutched the bag, full of tablets and herbs and hope, then nodded. It had to work.

It had to.

Nora talked cheerfully on our way home, filling up the gaps of silence with mindless chatter about her holiday plans. My fingers clutched the wheel more tightly as she spoke of visiting family outside London over Christmas. We'd never discussed what would happen over the holidays. I hadn't even been thinking about them, and now they were only a few weeks away. I shook my head, trying to rattle the days into place and realized with horror that I'd lost track of an entire week somehow. December had arrived and between Christmas photos, Bless news, and Nora coming to work, I'd lost track of time. Now Christmas was only ten days away, and I hadn't bought a single present, sent cards, or considered whether we should stay here or return to London. The only reason we even had a tree up was thanks to Smith's oversight.

"Are you going to be gone long?" I asked Nora in a tight voice. I was still adjusting to having her here. Now she was going to leave. A numb coldness spread through me at the thought of facing Christmas morning this year.

"A day or two," she said, quickly adding, "unless you need me here. I don't have to go."

I wasn't going to be the monster bitch boss that demanded her nanny work over the holidays, so I shook my head. "Just wondering. We'll have family around, so I'm just thinking ahead."

Nora had taken one of the two guest rooms, the one closest to Penny's nursery, as her own. That only left one room for visitors. Not that I had invited anyone down to stay. Undoubtedly, they all had plans at this point. I hadn't heard from any of them. Not even an invitation to join Clara and Alexander at Balmoral like we had done last year.

Last year? Christmas in Scotland seemed so very long ago. I'd been hoping to get pregnant then, filled with so much happiness over what the future held. It was hard to believe only a year ago I'd felt that way. It seemed like a distant memory now.

We pulled into Thornham's circular drive and parked. Between all the baby items I'd insisted we bring after our last disastrous outing, my packages from the pharmacy, and the baby herself, both of us had our hands full. As we reached the door, it swung open. I expected to see Humphrey rushing out to help us but was surprised when Smith stepped out in bare feet and took Penny from my arms.

"Allow me." He cradled her closely, kissing the top of her forehead. "Hello, beautiful."

His words, directed at our daughter, stung, and I immediately shrugged them off. Of course, he would call her that. She was beautiful. Penny was the prettiest baby I'd ever seen. It was completely normal.

"Waiting for us?" My eyes raked over him. He was in an

old pair of jeans and a loosely ribbed sweater. I spotted his dirty boots in the tray next to the door.

"Just finished up and saw you were on your way back," he said smoothly, leaning to give me a kiss.

I frowned. "Saw?"

"You were coming down the drive," he said, but his eyes didn't meet mine.

Smith was lying to me. I knew it as surely as I knew that I loved him—that he was my soul mate. The lie squeezed my heart, like it wanted to be seen for what it was. I just didn't understand why.

"How did it go?" he asked in an even tone, so perfectly calculated I wondered if he'd been planning this moment in his head all day.

"He gave me drugs." I held up the pharmacy bags. "They're going to fix me."

"That's all?" He sounded disappointed, and I wondered if he'd expected me to come back as a Stepford wife, suddenly prim and pleasing and poised.

"I'm supposed to take walks and ask for help," I bit out with a tired smile. Before I could finish, the door chime interrupted us. Smith had Penny and Nora had disappeared to put away her things, so I answered it just as Humphrey arrived to do the honors.

The detective who'd overseen the investigation into our cellar was on the other side. I shot Smith a quizzical look.

"The family is all here. I do believe you've added one to your number," he said in a jovial tone.

It took me a second to realize he was talking about Penny. I'd been pregnant the last time he was here. "Come in."

Humphrey looked even more put out that I'd invited the

detective inside the house, and he bustled up, offering to take his coat.

"I only came to speak with Mr. Price." He waved off the assistance. "But if this isn't a good time..."

"No, it's fine," he said.

I held out my arms to take the baby, wondering what this was about. Smith passed Penny to me before leading the police detective into the sitting room. He turned and smiled before he reached for the pocket doors that separated the space. As they slid shut, closing him off to me, I realized Smith wasn't just lying to me.

He was keeping secrets.

20

SMITH

"I am sorry to disturb you," Detective Longborn said, taking a seat on the sofa. He glanced around the room and nodded appreciatively at the holiday decorations. "It's nice to see this house with some life in it again. It's been a long time since anyone celebrated Christmas here."

"Thornham is a family home again," I said in a tight voice. Longhorn's timing couldn't have been worse. Not only had I forgotten to mention to Belle he'd be stopping by, he'd done so right as she was telling me about her doctor's appointment. Given how difficult it was to get her to open up these days, I couldn't help being concerned that my window to hear the details would be closed when I was done here. I didn't want to have to press Nora for information. I'd already slipped up and nearly admitted that I'd asked the nanny to send a message as soon as they were on the way home today.

"You said you had an update for me," I prompted, ready to get Longborn talking.

"Yes, but I'm afraid it's not good news."

I stopped, my eyes wandering to a nearby brass bar cart

and the crystal decanter sitting on it. I'd chosen to give up drinking a year ago. Since then, I found myself breaking that promise on more than one occasion. Generally, I did so out of a sense of social obligation. I couldn't help thinking that a detective delivering bad news about the bones in my basement was just such an occasion. "Drink?"

I half expected him to refuse, given that he was clearly on duty, but he nodded. Maybe, that's how things were here. It wasn't as though Briarshead had a high crime rate. Surely, a detective could have a drink in the afternoon with a local. Still, as I turned to pour one, I caught his eyes skittering nervously around the room. What did he have to tell me that had put him this on edge?

"Do you remember Christmases here?" I asked him.

"Before my time," he said. "But there's always someone in the village telling stories about Thornham's glory days."

"You say that like they're a thing of the past," I pointed out, pouring Macallan into a tumbler.

He gave an apologetic smile when I brought it to him. "I didn't mean to offend. It's hard to get used to seeing people living here. It's been vacant most of my life."

"Why is that?" Purchasing the estate had been easier than anticipated. It had been a surprise to find out that it had sat vacant for so long before it went up for sale. Despite that, the house hadn't been on the market for more than a few weeks when we purchased it.

"The remaining family didn't want to sell," he said with a shrug before taking a sip of his Scotch and sighing appreciatively. "You've got the good stuff."

If you only knew. I prided myself on having the good stuff. The biggest house. The prettiest wife. The best Scotch.

But having Longborn sitting here, reminded me that all those points of pride were an illusion. I had the biggest house, but I knew nothing about it. I didn't know why it sat empty for all of those years. I had the prettiest wife, but there was something ugly inside her, hurting her and I couldn't seem to root it out. In actuality, my Scotch seemed to be the only thing of value I could claim pride in.

"I assume this is about the bones." The time for pleasantries had passed. Longborn was going to keep avoiding the real reason he was here until I forced him to talk.

"I know when we first spoke, I said that it wouldn't be unusual to find something like this in a house of this age." His thumb skimmed along the cut-crystal edge of his glass.

I nodded. I thought the same thing. A house that had been standing since the 16th century had to come with its own history—both good and bad.

"Unfortunately, the laboratory results have come back and the bones aren't quite as old as we suspected."

"How old are they?" I asked slowly, already certain I didn't want to know the answer.

"A few decades," he said in a quiet voice, triggering my memory of what Georgia had said this afternoon on the phone.

"Does this have something to do with the closed case file you wouldn't release to my associate?" I asked coldly. I was losing patience with the village detective quickly. If he had come to deliver bad news, I was ready for him to have it out. I'd dealt with enough recently.

"We aren't in the habit of handing out closed case files to whoever calls." Longhorn's chest puffed out importantly, but his darting eyes told me that his confidence was a front.

"I think you'll find that Georgia Kincaid has the clearance to read any file she wants," I said flatly, adding, "as do I."

"Is that so?"

I didn't often use my connections to the royal family to my own advantage. But I was at my wits end with Thornham Park, Detective Longborn, and small-minded superstitions.

"She works as the Queen's private security," I told him.

His eyebrows shot up in surprise. He paused before taking a large gulp of Scotch. "And how are you connected to her?"

"I knew her first," I said. I didn't need to explain the makeshift family tree that branched around the Royal family. It wasn't a tree, so much as a tangle of vines. Invasive. Growing up and around as it pleased, strangling the lives out of some of its members, twisting around others, and caging the rest of us. An outsider simply wouldn't understand.

"And you have the same clearance?" Longborn said when I didn't continue.

"I do. I'm sure I can have someone call to prove it." For a moment, I considered asking Alexander to do just that. I would never have another problem with Longborn or the local officers if the king called to vouch for me. It was the kind of thing that would impress average men leading ordinary lives. Alexander did owe me one. He owed me a few. But I couldn't stomach the idea of using my connections to deal with this.

"I'll find it," Longborn said. "I'm afraid we're behind the times. Really, it's more of a hassle than anything."

I suddenly understood part of his hesitance. I was asking a man to do his job when he rarely had to rise to the occasion to do so. Most of his time was probably spent checking in on the local shops, responding to petty disturbances called in by old ladies, and meeting with the local town council. He didn't have to deal with bones and closed files and subsequent investigations into the matter by people associated with the Crown.

"I would appreciate it. But what does the age of the bones tell you?" I didn't want to forget to address it.

"There are always stories about houses this old. It's hard to know which ones are true. Most of them have been blown up over the years. They're old wives tales and stories we tell our kids on chilly nights to give them a good scare." Longborn stared into his glass before lifting his eyes. "But sometimes stories are true. The trick is knowing fact from fiction."

"The bones change the story," I guessed in a quiet voice.

"Perhaps," he admitted, heaving a sigh. "I don't know if there's a point to dragging up old crimes."

"It depends on the crime," I said.

"Will you feel that way if I have to tear apart your cellar?" he asked. "I can speak with the town council, reopen old investigations into disappearances around the estate."

"Disappearances?" This was only getting worse.

The last thing I wanted was to dredge up bad history. Now wasn't the time. I needed to focus on my wife and my family. But couldn't I just ignore what we'd found. "I'd like the file. I'll have my people look into it. I don't think there's cause to bring the town council into things."

Longborn smiled in understanding. He paused, his mouth opening but hesitated before he spoke.

"Unless that's a problem," I said, hoping to prompt him to share what was on his mind.

"Far be it for me, to tell a man how to run his home," he started, and I got the sense he was about to do just that, "but sometimes the past is better left in the past."

I often thought the same thing. But every time I tried to

move forward, it seemed the past stuck it's rotting hands out of the earth and dragged me back down to hell. Maybe there were no answers to be found where Thornham was concerned. Maybe I needed to remind myself that I'd never escape my own sins until I learned to let go of the past.

"I'll keep that in mind," I promised him. I didn't know what I was going to do when those files arrived or what they would contain. Maybe it would be best to simply pass them to Georgia and have her look into the matter. She had the benefit of distance where things were concerned.

I showed Longborn to the door. He paused at the entrance, taking his hat off the hook next to it and popping it on his head. "Thank you for the Scotch. Call me if you find any other strange discoveries."

"Should I expect to?" I asked him, puzzled over why he would bring that up.

"I imagine this house has more secrets inside it," he said simply. "Congratulations on your new baby. Give your wife my best. And Mr. Price, if you don't mind me saying so, keep an eye on them."

"I will."

He tipped his hat one more time before shoving his hands in his pockets and descending the steps towards an old Renault parked in the circle drive. My gaze followed behind him, wondering if his final words were simply good natured advice or a warning.

I shut the door behind him, my fingers glancing over the lock. It was the middle of the day. Humphrey and Mrs. Winters and Rowan would all be coming and going. I wasn't in London anymore where locking your door was second nature. There was no reason to need locked doors in a house this size, but Longborn's words lingered in the air around me. I drew my hand back, deciding that it was ridiculous to lock the door in the middle of the afternoon. Then, I went to look for Belle.

I found Nora with Penny in the nursery, rocking her softly. Daylight streamed around her, casting a shimmering glow. She looked up at me and smiled. I returned it and edged quietly out of the room. I appreciated having her here to help. I just couldn't quite get used to finding her with the baby. That would take time. A quick search of the bedroom yielded no results. I finally found Belle sitting behind my desk, chair turned to face the window overlooking the grounds.

"Waiting for me, beautiful?" I asked, repeating how she greeted me earlier.

She didn't respond, and I walked into the office toward her. As I reached the desk, I realized its drawers were open, a number of items strewn across the top of it, including my father's gun. It took me a moment to process what I was seeing. "Were you looking for something?"

"Not exactly."

I picked up the gun and placed it in the back of the center drawer. Then I did the same for a few files. My hands shook a little, rocked by finding her here with a gun so close by, even if it wasn't loaded. I couldn't shake the feeling she had been rummaging through my drawers for a reason.

"What are you looking for?" I asked.

"Whatever you're hiding," she said, her voice cracking.

"Hiding?" I had nothing to hide from Belle. My life was an open book to her. If only I could say the same about her. "I'm not hiding anything from you, beautiful."

I waited for her to respond.

"Hey, I mean it." I spun the leather chair around to discover her clutching a familiar frame in her hands.

"You weren't hiding this?" she asked, her lower lip trembling.

I should have tossed the photograph of Margot the day I found it. "I don't know how that got here," I said honestly. "I put it in a box."

"It was in your desk drawer," she said quietly.

I shook my head. That couldn't be right. I put it in the box myself. "It was," I admitted. "I'm not sure why you put it there. When I saw it, I threw it in an empty box to toss it."

"I didn't put it there," she said, her voice pitching up an octave. "I just found it there."

"I don't mean today." I had no idea how the photograph had gotten out of the box back and into my desk drawer. "When you were unpacking, you must've put it in the drawer."

"Why would I put a picture of your dead wife there?" Belle snapped.

"Why would you do anything?" I asked, losing my cool. Instantly, I regretted it. If Belle had been hurt before, now she was livid. She threw the photograph on the desk with such force the glass cracked, splintering around Margot's smile. "Oops. Sorry."

I ignored the edge of challenge in her voice. She wasn't the least bit sorry. Not that I cared about the damn photograph. "It should never have gotten here in the first place. I didn't realize I still had it. I'm sorry you found it."

"The first time or this time?" She pushed up from the chair, backing away from me as she shook her head. "I'm not crazy, Smith. I didn't put that in your drawer."

"You were the only one unpacking in here," I said. It didn't make any sense.

"I put a few books on the shelf." She crossed her arms over her chest protectively. "Your pens in your desk. I looked past the gun I found there. But I had nothing to do with your fucking photo. I won't make a mistake of digging into your secrets anymore, though. I wouldn't want you to have to be honest with me."

"Honest? Where is this coming from? I don't have anything to hide from you."

"How did you know I was coming home?" She leveled her blue eyes at me, and I knew I was caught. "I know you didn't see us coming up the drive."

It had been a bad lie, and I knew it at the time. If I had seen them, I would've stayed outside and helped her carry the baby in. Instead, she found me, shoes off, at the door. But being honest with her about that undermined my arrangement with Nora.

"Fine." She threw her hands in the air when I didn't confess. "Don't tell me. But don't tell me that you have no secrets either. You're keeping something from me."

She stormed out of the room, leaving me to stare after her. I didn't have secrets from my wife.

But—I did.

I didn't regret asking Nora to give me updates, especially given that Belle had resisted opening up to me herself. She hadn't been honest with me about that day at the restaurant. I'd given her plenty of time to tell me. I could live with the intention of those lies. But what about Longborn and the bones? Belle didn't want to be at Thornham. That much was clear. But I wasn't certain our problems could be solved by going back to London. And, try as I might, I couldn't forget the sinister gift she'd received at her baby shower. No one had claimed responsibility for that. There'd been no follow-up. All I could do was understand the message as it was intended when it was sent. In London we were so tangled in the royal family's vines, that the dangerous weeds that grew into them, bastardizing them even more, could always reach us. As long as we stayed there in Alexander and Clara's orbit, we would never be free of our pasts. We would never make our own choices. We would always be in danger for standing by the ones we loved. I owed more to Belle and Penny than a life like that. It's why I couldn't tell her about the bones. Not until I'd seen the file and what was inside it. Maybe everything had been blown out of proportion. The bones were decades old, he said. But that could be twenty years or ninety years. That made a difference. There was no point upsetting her further until I knew more, not while I couldn't seem to reach her at even the most basic levels.

That was the real problem. I'd lost my grip on Belle before, watching her slip away from me after she lost our first child to miscarriage. I hadn't been enough to comfort her then. Now? I was losing her once more. I didn't want to. I just didn't know how to reach her.

I glanced at the shattered picture of Margot and shook my head. Reaching for it, I threw it across the room. It hit the wall, the already broken glass tinkling to the ground as the frame cracked into two separate pieces.

Was it even possible to learn from past mistakes? I thought we had everything. Too much, even. We'd had to decide what we wanted. That's how we'd wound up here in the country with Penny. But somewhere along the line I'd made the wrong decision. I'd calculated based on certain assumptions, and now I needed to backtrack until I figured out where I'd gone wrong. I only knew one thing: I had to reach Belle before it was too late.

I couldn't wait any longer.

My feet carried me in the direction she left. Somehow, I knew I wouldn't find her in the nursery. It broke my heart to see her struggle with Penny. I needed to remind her that she was enough. More than that, she was *everything*. When I walked into the bedroom, she didn't look up from where she sat at the edge of the bed.

I sat next to her, running my hands down her arms as I leaned to kiss her shoulder. Belle turned in to me, without a word. I cupped her chin with my palm and brought her lips to mine. We needed to find our way back to each other. She had to feel the same.

Hooking my arm around her, I guided her onto her back.

"I want you," I told her, moving to stand between her legs. I drew off her pants and her eyes shuddered to a close.

Her legs butterflied open as I yanked my dick out. We didn't have all the answers, but we had this. We had each other. I thrust inside her, earning a soft grunt. It had been too long since I felt my wife. Belle grabbed the edge of the bed as I urged her legs up to coil around my waist.

But I needed more. I needed to feel her, kiss her. I needed my skin on her skin. My lips on her lips.

I withdrew and her legs closed ever so briefly as I pushed her up on the bed. They opened again as I climbed over her and joined her again. I rocked slowly inside her, wanting to reawaken this part of our love gently. We'd begun our relationship violently, taking with a hunger that had turned to obsession. Now we had the rest of our lives to enjoy one another. I wanted to savor that.

"You feel amazing," I murmured, lowering my mouth to kiss her.

She accepted my lips, but she didn't respond. I pulled back, holding my body over her with one arm and bringing my finger to trace her face.

"Is this okay? We can go slower."

Belle arched up and kissed me again, but there was nothing passionate about it. It was mechanical and forced and I found myself slowing down as I tried to understand. Maybe gently wasn't the way to bring us back together. I increased my pace, hammering against her and calling her to me.

"Come for me," I urged. "Show me."

Her eyes opened and the flash of blue released me, but as I emptied inside her, it wasn't Belle staring back at me. But where she should be, there was nothing but a hollow void.

I rolled off her, reaching to hold her but she turned away and made herself small, tugging her knees to her chest. I felt sick. My fingers brushed her shoulder.

"I love you."

There was no response.

I stayed like that until I was certain she was asleep. It was all I could. I wasn't even sure she wanted me there, at all.

I went back to my office, defeated, knowing exactly what I had to do. I dialed Edward's number, uncertain he would answer. He'd gone to even greater lengths than me to separate himself from the Royals. He answered on the third ring.

"She needs you," I said.

"What's wrong?"

"She's lost, and I can't find her." I sank into the chair,

burying my face in my hand. "I'm scared there won't be anything left of her to find soon."

There was a pause. He had a decision to make. But we both knew there was no real choice. "I'll be there as soon as I can get a flight."

I hung up with him, hoping that whenever that was, it wouldn't be too late.

21

SMITH

We had barely spoken over the past three days. At night, Belle turned away from me in bed. Thornham also had a fatal flaw that I hadn't foreseen until then. It was easy to hide on the estate's sprawling grounds. It seemed I was constantly *just missing* Belle. I'd grown tired of Nora's sympathetic smiles when she told me that Belle had gone out for a walk or Mrs. Winters pursed lips as she shook her head every time I asked if she'd seen my wife.

"Lost her again?" she said with disapproval, shaking her head and turning back to the shepherd's pie she was making for dinner.

My frustration had shifted into uneasy guilt. For the first time, I found myself questioning my intimate relationship with my wife. When I looked back on the other night, I no longer saw it as me trying to reach her, but as a man being too arrogant to realize he wasn't wanted. Was that why she had been so distant? Was that why looking into her eyes had felt like staring into the bottomless depths of the ocean?

I missed my wife. I loved my wife. I just didn't know how to find her.

"We're going to have a guest at dinner," I told Mrs. Winters. She huffed, beginning to complain under her breath about not getting any warning as she continued preparing the evening meal. I left her there, still muttering. I felt somehow that without complaining, she wouldn't know what to do with her time. Every night she made enough food for an army. Belle hardly ate anything these days, picking at her plate like a bird. We always had leftovers. The most trouble she would have to go to was to add a seat at the newly arrived dining table.

I gave up trying to find Belle. My wife could hide from me. I would let her if that's what she needed to do to process this. Something told me that she'd be coming to me sooner rather than later, though.

That afternoon after consulting with Rowan about the project in the back, I decided to grab a quick shower before driving into town to pick up Penny's Christmas present. I stepped into the shower, turning on the water to rinse off the dirt from outdoors. One thing I hadn't counted on when we moved to the country was how much goddamn labor it would take to get the place up to scratch. I leaned forward planting my palms against the tiled wall and let the hot water run down my sore neck and shoulders. I'd kept in shape in London, lifting weights and running, but exercise meant to offset the city lifestyle hadn't prepared me for the rigors of manual labor. Honestly, it felt good. Building something with my hands, making this home for my family? It was one of the most fulfilling things I'd ever done, even if it hurt like a bitch.

As good as it felt, I didn't have much time if I was going to make it into the village before dark. The days had grown shorter as Christmas drew nearer. Each morning, I woke expecting to find snow, but nothing had fallen yet. Instead, by the time four in the afternoon rolled around, the sky began to darken. In the country, the darkness was so heavy it felt like you could slice through it with a knife.

I shampooed my hair quickly and rinsed. As I turned off the water, I heard footsteps on the tile.

Despite everything, marriage had turned me into an optimist because I couldn't keep myself from calling out to Belle as I rubbed my face dry with a towel, "You're too late, beautiful. But I could be convinced to turn the shower back on if you want to join me."

The answer gasp and the voice that followed wasn't Belle's.

"Shit! I'm sorry!" Nora said.

I dropped the towel from my face, wrapping it around my waist in one motion, as I looked over to discover the nanny, standing frozen to the spot. She was gawking at me. Another time and in another life, I might have appreciated her obvious interest, but every part of me belonged to Belle now.

"What are you doing in here?" I roared, a primal rage taking over me.

That was enough to snap her out of her daze. She looked away quickly, beginning to back-up. "Belle was looking for... Sorry!"

Whatever it was must not have been important, or I must have scared her badly, because she turned and ran from the bathroom.

That was just what I needed. I stalked out of the shower, already canceling my plans to go into the village. There was no way, given the current state of things between my wife and I, that I was going to chance her hearing about this little encounter from anyone else, especially Nora. It had been innocent. A mistake. But I was a man walking on eggshells at the best of times. I might have no interest in Nora, but Belle had pointed out she found the nanny beautiful. I could only imagine how twisted this could become in her head, especially after the photograph of Margot.

I threw on a pair of trousers and a thick sweater ribbed with marled brown wool. I didn't even bother running a brush through my hair or finding shoes. Hopefully, Belle hadn't gone on another one of her sodding walks. I tore out of the closet, stopping dead in my tracks when I found her waiting for me by the bed.

"In a hurry?" she asked, arching an eyebrow.

"I was looking for you," I told her.

"In the closet?"

"Listen, beautiful," I said hurriedly, in no mood to have this turned into another argument. "I was grabbing a quick shower when you sent Nora in for whatever it was you needed. I don't want you to think anything happened."

"Did something happen?"

"No," I repeated. "I just wanted you to know that it happened."

"But you just said nothing happened," she said.

She was fucking infuriating. It was making me hard. "Yes. I mean, no. Jesus Christ, Belle, what do you want?"

"Some lotion, actually." She abandoned her interrogation, strolling into the bathroom to dig in a vanity drawer. As she came out, she waved the bottle. "This is what I sent Nora in for."

"Maybe advise her to knock next time," I said dryly, stretching an arm toward her. Belle was in a surprisingly good mood—playful even.

She stepped backward, dashing my illusions about the situation. "She told me what happened. It sounded like an accident."

"It was an accident." I frowned, wondering if she was going to ever let me touch her again. I wasn't being punished for the thing with Nora. This was about something else. The other night? Or had I fucked up worse than that?

"In that case..." Belle started toward the door.

"Are you going to keep punishing me?" I called after her before I could stop myself.

"You didn't do anything wrong, remember?"

The dismissiveness of her tone needled me. No, I hadn't done anything wrong, but that wasn't going to stop her from continuing to give me the cold shoulder. Until I could get her to admit what was bothering her, I had no hope of actually doing anything to change it. But if she was going to persist in believing that I was keeping pictures of my dead wife in my desk or that I enjoyed having a young, beautiful nanny around the house, I didn't know what I could do about it. I'd gotten rid of Margot's picture. I had no interest in Nora. Did I need to fire her and hire some old woman from the village? I would do anything if it meant Belle would be happy again.

"If you think—" the chime of the front door cut her off mid sentence. She groaned, throwing back her head. "We've been getting deliveries all day. Jane sent something. Clara and Alexander sent gifts."

"Your friends miss you," I said carefully. "We never talked about going back to London for Christmas."

"Everyone has plans by now," she snapped, turning on her heel to walk out of the room. I was two steps behind her when a familiar, and very welcome, voice floated up the staircase from the landing below.

"Is this the welcome I receive? Usually I expect a parade."

Belle's head whipped around to me, surprise on her face and one name on her lips. "Edward?"

"I thought you needed your best friend," I said, the words tasting bitter on my tongue. I swallowed against the sourness I felt, reminding myself that I would do anything for her, even if I wasn't the one she really wanted. I stepped past her, brushing one hand across her forearm. "I wish I could give you everything you need."

We stared at one another for a moment, me searching her eyes hoping to catch a glimpse of the woman who felt so far from me now. She looked at me, her expression unreadable, before her eyelids shuddered close, and she whispered. "You have. Thank you."

Something broke inside me. I'd given her what she needed, delivered her best friend—someone she might actually talk to—but the victory felt hollow. I wanted to be that person for her. Until the last few weeks, I thought I was that person. We lingered there for a moment, hearing the faint welcomes of Humphrey and Mrs. Winters, acknowledging Edward's arrival below us. Finally, Belle turned and started toward the stairs. Without thinking, my hand lashed out, grabbing hers. "Find your way back to me, beautiful."

She opened her mouth, but then her teeth descended into her lower lip, and she continued down the stairs without a word.

22

BELLE

"Warning, Mrs. Winters can be a little testy," I said under my breath.

Edward gave me a crooked smile. "You forget I was the peacekeeper in my family growing up. No one can resist my charms."

I seriously doubted that, but I couldn't help noticing how much more relaxed Edward seemed since his return home from Italy. He'd filled me in on his time away. Most of it he'd spent on the Riviera or bouncing about Tuscany in search of the best wine. Somehow, he'd even managed to stay incognito enough that no one recognized him. I still had a hard time believing that. Maybe people there were just less interested in the scandals surrounding his family.

As we sat down around the new dining table, it was clear that he intended to make good on his promise to win Mrs. Winters's affection over dinner. When she sat the large shepherd's pie in the center of the table, he whistled appreciatively.

"I missed real food," he told her. "I think I've had enough noodles for a lifetime."

"Well, it doesn't show," she said, eyeing him with a mixture of suspicion and pride. "But I'll be glad to cook any of your favorites while you're here."

She bustled back towards the kitchen, humming happily to herself. She was still determined her place was there and ours was here in the formal dining room, but I'd never seen her look so self-satisfied. Edward tossed a wink in my direction as if to say *see?*

"She's always asking me what I want to eat," I said with a shrug, feeling my own lips tugging up.

"That's because you're the lady of the house," he said, unfolding a napkin and placing it in his lap. "You're supposed to dictate the menu."

"As though I care what we eat. Who would? I'm just happy to be fed."

"Clara made the same complaint when they moved to Buckingham." The statement was out of his mouth before he realized what he was saying. A gloomy silence descended instantly over the table, and I found myself shooting Smith a look, hoping he could think of something—*anything*—to say that would change the topic.

"Will you stay for Christmas?" Smith asked.

I was a little surprised they hadn't hashed out more of the details before he arrived. I'd assumed this was part of Smith's gift to me, convincing Edward to finally visit for the holidays.

"I don't want to impose, but I was well past due to meet little Penny." He dug his fork into the potatoes on his plate, moving them around a bit without taking a bite. "I'm here as long as you want."

"Careful," Smith warned him, "she'll never let you leave."

Even though he smiled as he spoke, I didn't miss the sharp edge biting through his words. Edward, however, seemed blissfully ignorant to the double meaning hiding under Smith's statement.

"The place is big enough," he said. "I'd love to stay for Christmas if you'll have me."

It was the best news I'd received in weeks. "You can help me shop for Christmas. With everything going on, I haven't even started."

"Of course you haven't," he said with a laugh, as though this was perfectly natural. "You just had a baby. You have a new house. Honestly, if you know what day of the week it is, you're killing it."

A flash of gratitude crossed Smith's face, but he turned his attention to his plate as soon as he realized I saw.

"I think this is the best thing she's made," he said conversationally.

"I'll have to ask her to teach me how to cook it," Edward said.

My fork froze midway to my mouth. "Excuse me?"

"How to cook it," he repeated. "The recipe?" he added when I continued to stare at him.

"I was fairly certain you didn't know how to boil an egg," I told him.

"I'm not that helpless."

I placed my fork on the table and leveled my face to his in challenge. "So you know how to boil an egg?"

"I could learn," he said with a wave of his hand. "It didn't come up in my cooking class."

"Cooking class?" I repeated, even more shocked.

"What do you think I was doing in Italy?" he asked.

"I don't know." I shrugged. Not learning to cook. "Staring at beautiful Italian men and sipping spritzes?"

"It turns out you can only do that for so many hours in a day," he said dryly. "I figured if I'm going to strike out on my own, I'm going to need to know how to do things like cook."

There was a brief moment of tense silence as I realized what he was implying. I glanced at Smith, seeing the same understanding written across his face.

"That makes sense," I said swiftly, worried the conversation would veer into dangerous territory. This was the first Edward had talked about plans that lasted more than a holiday trip to whatever part of the globe caught his fancy. I didn't want to press him too far too fast, but it was nice to see him thinking about the future, even if I wasn't sure I liked the implication of him striking out on his own. "So, Christmas shopping? I have no idea if Briarshead has decent shops."

"I'm sure it's not Harrods," he said, "but we can find something. Smith must need hunting gear or golf equipment or whatever manly hobby he's taking up in the countryside."

"I'm quite busy enough," my husband said in a clipped tone. "I'd rather you two just enjoyed yourself and not worry about me."

I couldn't help wondering if Smith had even bothered getting me a Christmas present. Maybe that's why he didn't want me to shop for him. It was not as though there'd been time, and neither of us had been to London since Penny was born. He was always here, always working, always overseeing some new project on the grounds. I made up my mind not to stress about a present for him. If something caught my eye, I'd pick it up. Otherwise a new baby and a new house seemed like more than enough for one year.

In the meantime, Edward had drawn out his mobile to check the Internet for the shops available to us in the village. As he began to fill me in, ranking his interest and making slightly snide remarks about a few of them, I found myself laughing. After a few minutes, I felt Smith's eyes on me. Looking up, I found a stony mask in place of a smile. He'd worn it often when we first met, guarding himself from me. Now it was back. He'd been the one to call Edward here, so why was he acting so coldly? Before I could hunt for more clues, he laid his napkin on the table and rose.

"If you'll excuse me. I need to return a few phone calls," he said "I'll check on Penny."

"We can do that," Edward said quickly. "I want to spend more time with my godchild. I assume I'm her godfather?"

"I'll put it in the will," Smith said dryly. "Good night." He disappeared into the hall, off to do whatever he did in his study in the evenings. The memory of opening his desk drawer to find Margot's photograph drifted into my mind, and I shooed it away.

Tonight, I was determined to be happy. That was the first step in finding my way back to him.

EDWARD'S GOOD MOOD HAD CONTINUED INTO THE following day. When I brought up Christmas shopping, he'd insisted we go, and that we bring Penny along. *Just the two of us.* I'd battled my own anxiety over it and agreed. For the last hour we'd been strolling through Briarshead, popping in and out of the small shops in the village. Most of them required we leave the pram at the door, given the age of the buildings and their layouts, so Edward took to carrying Penny. He was a natural at it, and it was clear Penny adored her Uncle Edward.

"Spill," I demanded. "What's your secret?"

He turned, Penny cradled in one arm asleep, and a book in his other hand. "I'm sorry?"

"You're clean-shaven, well-dressed, and in a good mood," I said, crossing my own arms and studying him like I might be able to unlock what was going on with or without his assistance.

"And that's a problem?" he asked

I hesitated, worried that bringing David up might ruin the festive atmosphere. The truth was I was desperate to know how he was doing it. The last time I'd seen Edward, he'd been in a dark place. Had Italy been that amazing? Part of me had thought when he arrived that there would be someone to share my misery with. Instead, I'd gotten my best friend delivered to me in one cleaned up, cheerful package. "The last time I saw you..."

"Some things have changed since then," he said quietly, placing the book back on the shelf. "Some things haven't."

"What changed?" I asked, not trying to hide the plea in my voice. Edward hadn't simply come for Christmas. He'd been summoned by Smith, which meant he'd been filled in on what was going on in my life. He knew about the postpartum depression. I was sure of it. If he had some secret cure that could fix me, I wanted to know.

"I started taking pills," he said, hurriedly adding, "prescription ones, I mean. I spoke to a doctor. I just decided I didn't want to feel that way."

A lump formed in my throat. That was his secret? I blinked against a sudden blur of tears. I'd already tried that.

"Hey, talk to me. I get the sense that's not what you wanted to hear." Edward stepped closer, giving us a little bit of privacy. Now that he had cleaned up his act, eyes followed him all over the village. He was no longer flying under the radar. Briarshead knew Prince Edward was in town.

"I went to the doctor," I whispered, "and I started the medication, but it just makes me sleepy and fuzzy."

He pushed the bridge of his horn rimmed glasses higher up on his nose, nodding thoughtfully. "When did you start taking it?"

"A few days ago," I said.

"It takes a fortnight at least," he said soothingly. "You just have to give them time to work."

"Are they going to make me feel this terrible forever?" I asked.

"I didn't have side effects, but I read the pamphlet the pharmacist gave me," he said with a grin. "I think you'll be okay. If you're not feeling better by the time two weeks is passed, maybe you should talk to your doctor about something else."

I had the oddest sensation that I'd found myself in some type of advertisement: *Talk to your doctor about this medication or that medication or anything that might take your hot mess and turn it into the polished, poised woman you'd once been.* I forced a smile.

"Don't do that with me," he said firmly. "I know when you're over-thinking."

"Would you rather I just cried?" I asked as we stepped out of the bookshop, and Edward carefully deposited Penny in her pram, wrapping several layers of blanket around her. She stirred, momentarily opening sleepy eyes to find him smiling back at her. It was enough to reassure her, and she fell back asleep.

"I'd rather you be happy," he admitted. "I think that's what Smith wants, too. The first step is going to have to be admitting that you aren't. You can't fake it until you make it when you're depressed."

He put an arm around my shoulder and pulled me close.

"I want to be happy," I said softly.

"That's the first step, love." He pressed a kiss to the side of my head.

"What's the next one?"

"Take it one day at a time," he advised, "and when it's all too much, chocolate never fails."

"I know just the place to take you," I said.

We continue down the main street, shifting to light-hearted banter about the items for sale in shop windows. The truth was that having him here had done more good for my soul than I thought possible. But I couldn't hang all the responsibility of feeling better on him. Not when he had his own life to get back to.

"What about Smith?" Edward asked.

"I didn't get him anything this year, except a baby," I said absently.

"No, not that. How is Smith feeling about things? He seemed worried when he called me." Apparently, Edward wasn't going to avoid difficult conversations. He'd really meant that he wanted to help me. I suspected, he felt he learned his lesson the hard way in regards to things like that.

"He's fine. He adores the baby. She adores him."

"And?" Edward pressed.

I shrugged. "What else matters?"

"You two usually can't keep your hands off each other," he said meaning "Last night you barely looked at each other."

"What did you say? Some things have changed?" My words were hollow, but coated with the bitterness I felt towards the situation.

"Now I'm really worried," he said. "Do you want to talk about it?"

"It's just that everything's different," I confessed. "I'm not very good at this whole mum thing. I'm sure you heard."

"I only heard that you are stressed. No one—including Smith—said a thing about your skills as a mother. Besides, it's not like it's not a huge transition. Would you start any new job and expect to be good at it on the first day?"

"I'm pretty sure that's exactly what it's supposed to be like when you become a mum." At least that's how it felt to me. "Look at Clara."

"Clara has nothing else to do," Edward muttered. "My brother sees to that."

"She's a good mum," I said, shifting the conversation away from Alexander and back to my original point. I'd unintentionally hit his sore spot. But if he was going to force me to confront the ugly things I tried to hide inside myself, then I needed to do the same for him.

He hesitated. "She is."

"Do you want to talk about it?" I asked him. We'd skirted around the topic the last time I saw him in London. Then, he'd been simmering on a low boil, any moment I'd expected him to explode. It was there under the surface all the time. I no longer sensed that. That didn't mean that every time the conversation touched on his brother or his late husband, I didn't spy some of that undercurrent of anger, though.

"I'm trying to make peace with the fact that I'll never know why," he said in a gruff voice. "I don't think there's anything else I can do."

"You started to tell me something," I said thoughtfully as we paused so I could adjust Penny's blanket and double check to be sure that the pram's canopy blocked any possible wind. Her cheeks were slightly rosy, but all indications were that she was warm enough. "You said that the worst part was that sometimes and then Smith showed up before you could tell me."

"I'll confess if you will," he said.

"What do I have to confess?" I asked.

"I won't pretend that I'm healed or that I'm over it. I am happy sometimes now. Other days, I don't want to get out of bed," he admitted to me. "The most important thing I did was I stopped keeping all of the terrible thoughts I had locked away." He paused, giving me a pointed look as we reached the Briar Rose Inn.

"Do you want me to tell you all my crazy thoughts?"

"It's a good sign that you see them as crazy. That means that you don't believe them," he murmured. "But yes. I promise I won't judge you."

I glanced at Penny sleeping peacefully in her pram and wondered if that were true or if it was a pretty lie we told each other? That you loved them unconditionally. That you would never think less of them. But how true could that actually be?

How often was that kind of promise tested? The truth was that most of the time people didn't test those boundaries. They pleased their parents. They apologized. They made up with their spouse instead of holding on to anger. As much as I wanted to believe that humans were capable of that kind of unconditional acceptance, I knew we were also capable of holding grudges.

"Like you don't judge Alexander?"

Edward's eyes flashed, but before he could spit out whatever had boiled over inside him, Tomas opened the door to the restaurant.

"Are you going to stand out there with that baby or come inside?" he asked, waving us in the restaurant.

The momentary distraction gave both of us a moment to cool off as we got Penny out and carried her inside, parking the pram at the door.

"Hello," Tomas said, sticking out his hand to Edward. "I'm Tomas. Belle's favorite person in Briarshead."

"You're the only person I know in Briarshead," I reminded him.

"As I said, at the top, no?"

"Edward." He took Tomas's outstretched hand and shook it, but I spotted the bit of hesitation on his face. Edward waited for the moment of recognition, but Tomas continued on obliviously.

"In for a visit?" Thomas asked as he showed us to what he called the best seat in the house. Given that the house was empty, any seat would do. I couldn't help worrying a little that despite Tomas's obvious talent, the villagers of Briarshead didn't appreciate the restaurant for what it could offer them.

"I just got back into town," Edward said a bit dryly, he

shot me a look over Tomas's shoulder as if to say *is this really happening?*

"Staying for the holidays?"

"Yeah, although not sure there will be much excitement," Edward said, directing his teasing at me. "My best friend suddenly spends all day with the baby and falls asleep by nine. It's not going to be quite the same holiday season as last year."

I waited for Edward to piece together what he had just said. Every time Christmas and the holidays had come up there was a momentary pause, and even though he didn't always say anything, I knew he was thinking of last year. Life had been different then. We'd been in Scotland planning his surprise wedding to David. Now David was gone and he'd left a legacy of tragedy in his wake. But whether Edward was too distracted—puzzling out if Tomas was purposefully playing dumb or really didn't know who he was— his good mood seemed to return.

"Well, if you get bored, come down here and have a pint with me," Tomas offered. "The village does tend to settle down in the evenings, but there's a pub that stays open late enough. It's warm. Although the food's not as good as mine, so you might have to convince me to open the kitchen back up if we drink too much."

"Speaking of." I took the chance to interrupt whatever was happening between the two of them. "Can we have some of those stuffed dates?"

"Coming right up, but I'm choosing the rest of your meal," Tomas said mischievously.

"But I wanted the fish and chips," I said in a dry voice.

His only answer was a groan as he stomped back to the kitchen, pretending to be upset.

Across from me, Edward raised an eyebrow.

"His culinary skills are lost on the people here," I explained to my friend. "Also, the first time I met him, I thought he was flirting with me, but..."

"He just asked me out for a drink," Edward said, grinning despite himself.

"I've been out of the game too long," I said, shaking my head. "I didn't realize he's gay."

"You're just distracted," he said reassuringly. "You mistook his obvious good taste and thus interest in you for being *interested in you*."

"Is that it?" I found myself laughing. That was a mistake, because Penny stirred, letting out a kitten-like cry of frustration before burying her nose back and forth in Edward's shoulder.

"I think that means she wants you," he said, passing her to me.

It took a couple of tries to get her on the breast. She seemed more frustrated than usual, leaving me feeling frustrated as well. But having Edward with me made it easier. He distracted me by telling me ridiculous stories about his time in Italy. It turns out that while he took a cooking class, he couldn't claim to be a good cook by any measurable standard. In fact, judging from the stories, he seemed to have a natural aversion to cooking.

Tomas joined us, bringing a half dozen artfully arranged dates, wrapped in bacon, on a plate. He paused to take a seat to listen to the end of a disastrous tale that involved Edward mistaking sugar for salt in a recipe.

"I think you better let me do the cooking," he said.

"What about me?" I asked, finally relaxed as Penny nursed.

"You're too fabulous to cook," Tomas said with the air of a man who recognized such things. "If you don't have a cook of your own, I'll come to be your cook."

"I don't think Mrs. Winters is going anywhere," I said.

"Abigail?" Tomas repeated. "I didn't know she took a position."

"You know her?" It was a silly thing to ask. Of course he knew her. Everyone knew everyone in Briarshead. That was what happened when you lived in a small village.

"Sure," he said. "The Winters family has lived here nearly as long as my family has. She went off for a while, worked at some houses in London, and then she came back here. She definitely keeps to herself."

"Unless she has an opinion on what you're doing," I said dryly.

"I think you'll find most of the people in the village will let you know if they have an opinion on what you're doing." He smirked as he stood up. "I better go get lunch going. I need to make sure he eats. It sounds better if we don't allow him to cook."

As soon as he disappeared to the back, I waggled my eyebrows at Edward. "What do you think?"

"About what?"

"He's cute," I pressed. He was more than cute, Tomas was hot. I thought he was attractive the first time I'd met him, but suffering under the delusion that he was hitting on me had left me careful to keep my eyes to myself. Since I found out there was no harm, I could take a better look. "You two would be adorable together."

Edward answered with a tight smile. "I'm not ready for that."

"Sorry," I said, instantly feeling terrible. "That was insensitive of me."

"I guess there's no right way or wrong way to do this. It's not like I can tell you when I'll be ready," he said, suddenly sounding glum. "I won't know until I am."

"Until then, I'll go for a pint with you anytime," I offered.

"I might go for a quick drink," Edward said, the hint of a smile on his lips. "Especially if he's willing to cook for me. He's right. I'm totally rubbish at it."

We spent the rest of the afternoon catching up. As we finished the gigantic slice of chocolate cake Tomas brought us before disappearing to prep dinner, Edward poked at a few crumbs with his fork.

"I think I would've forgiven him," he said in a quiet voice.

"What?" I asked, not sure I heard him correctly.

"You asked me what I was going to say that day in London. That's the worst part," he admitted. "I think I would've forgiven him if he told me. I would've tried to help. I don't know what I could've done. I keep thinking about it. Why didn't he tell me?"

"Maybe he didn't want to put you in that situation," I offered gently. I scooped a bit of chocolate frosting onto my fork and deposited it in my mouth. We might need a second slice of cake for this discussion.

"I tell myself that. I tell myself that he wanted to tell me. But it doesn't change the fact that he didn't. It doesn't change what he did to Clara or Alexander. It doesn't change what he was willing to do to William." Edward swallowed hard. "That's why I can't see them. Because I'm angry that I didn't get to say goodbye to my husband. I'm angry because Alexander took him from me. But I also feel guilty every time I think about my nephew. I should've known. I should have protected him and Clara. What would've happened if they hadn't found her?"

I reached a hand across the table taking his in mine and squeezed it. "But they did find them," I said in a soft voice. "They're healthy. They're safe. You can't punish yourself for the choices that he made. And you should never, ever feel badly for loving someone, even if they didn't deserve you. That's their mistake, not yours."

I knew a thing or two about loving someone who saw themselves as irredeemable. I'd watched Smith struggle to become the man he was today. But I didn't just learn to love him despite the beast inside him, I learned to love the beast, too.

"I kinda think you need to take your own advice," Edward said meaningfully.

"I do now, huh?" I shifted, moving Penny onto my other shoulder.

"Stop beating yourself up. Stop punishing yourself. And stop punishing Smith."

"I don't see what that has to do with—"

"You're punishing him for loving you," Edward murmured. "I can see it. You're hurting. You're not yourself. I have faith that you're going to find yourself again. So does Smith. That's why he called me. He would do anything for you.

"He's keeping secrets from me," I told him.

"Word of advice? Just ask him about them," Edward said. "Don't make that mistake. And stop believing the lies your depression is telling you. You deserve love. You deserve magic. You deserve the happily-ever-after."

I wanted that to be true more than anything. Maybe I couldn't believe it now, but I was determined to find my way back to myself, to Smith, to Penny. Because I wanted my happily-ever-after, and I was ready to fight for it.

23

SMITH

After another dinner, it was clear that Edward had been right about winning over Mrs. Winters. His praise of her roast chicken had actually made her blush, and he was either talking a good game about learning how to cook or he meant it. I couldn't be sure which.

Since his arrival, the atmosphere in the house felt lighter. I couldn't deny that he'd put everyone in a good mood, particularly my wife.

Part of me resented the easy banter he had with Belle. It felt like a lifetime since I'd heard her laugh. But that was only a small, petty piece of me. Honestly, I was relieved. Nora had left to spend Christmas with her family and would be gone for a few days, so I rose as Mrs. Winters came to clear the plates and announced my intention to go check on Penny.

Before I could step away from the table, Edward jumped up, glaring at Belle "Let me do it," he said. "I haven't gotten enough one-on-one time with the new girl in my life."

"I've got it." I waved off the offer. I'd asked him to come

here to look after Belle, and he was doing an excellent job of it. I couldn't expect him to fill in for the nanny, too.

But to my surprise, Belle piped up.

"I wouldn't fight him on it," she told me. "He thinks Penny hung the moon, and I'm pretty sure she thinks Uncle Edward is the moon."

This wasn't news to me. The two of them had spent the last couple of days popping about town, coming home with arms loaded with packages, and I hadn't heard a whisper of trouble despite the fact that they took the baby almost every trip. Maybe Edward had a magic touch that extended not only to his best friend, but to our daughter, as well. I found myself grateful that he was here, even though Belle preferred his company to my own.

"Are you certain?" There had to be something a grown man wanted to do more than babysit.

Edward headed toward the door, pausing to clap one hand on my shoulder. He leaned closer, lowering his voice to a whisper, "I think you two could use some alone time."

I wasn't sure if it was a suggestion or a threat. Alone time with my wife sounded incredible. Too good to be true, really. Of course, it was just as likely that she wanted to have it out with me in private. I wasn't certain that Edward was in the mood to fix many marital issues these days so it was hard to know.

He reached down and swiped the baby monitor from the table. "I've got this." He waved it at us before heading out of the dining room towards the stairs.

After he'd gone, I stood, feeling foolish, as I waited for Belle to tell me what she expected. I had no idea when this had happened to us. It didn't seem that long ago that we were going about our lives, colliding together with passion at night or whenever we found a spare second, and working together towards a shared vision of our future. Now, I found myself uncertain of what step to take. I didn't want to scare her away. I didn't want to hurt her more than she was already hurting. I couldn't handle another moment of seeing her in pain.

Belle remained silent for a moment, and I could see wheels turning behind her eyes. She hadn't planned this, that much was clear. Edward had put her on the spot. Now she had to decide what to do. Finally, she stood, adjusting her cashmere sweater, her eyes trained on the floor. She didn't say anything. Instead, she crossed the room. I expected her to leave. Apparently we still weren't on speaking terms. But rather than go directly to the doorway, she paused and extended her hand.

I cocked my head, sending an unspoken question: was she sure?

Her hand remained out, and I took it. Neither of us spoke as we climbed the stairs. When we reached the top, we could hear Edward singing to Penny in the nursery. Belle smiled before pulling me towards our bedroom.

I'd taken charge for most of our relationship, but tonight, I allowed her to lead me to our bed. I wouldn't make assumptions. I wouldn't make mistakes. I couldn't risk pushing her any farther away from me than she already was.

"You got me here, beautiful. Now what are you going to do with me?" I asked her. I still didn't move.

Belle's eyes narrowed into slants before her palms spread across my chest. There was a longing to the touch that I recognized, but almost as quickly, she threw her weight behind them, pushing me down onto the mattress. I watched greedily as she climbed onto my lap, straddling my groin. Her arm looped around my neck, her fingers tangling in my hair before yanking my head back. Belle lowered her face over mine, her lips a breath away, close enough to kiss—and still I waited.

"You seem to suddenly be inflicted with patience," she purred.

"I just want to be whatever you need me to be," I said gruffly.

"Then be my man," she commanded, leaving no doubt of what she wanted.

She didn't have to ask twice. The hands I'd kept at my sides lashed out grabbing her by the hips and flipping her onto the bed. I'd made love to her the other night, gently calling her back to me. Why had I thought that would work? We had to fight like hell for each other and that's what made us unbreakable—our love was forged in fire. We needed this. We needed the hard. We needed to show each other that we could take it all again and again and again. I jerked her sweater up, not bothering to pull it off entirely, which left her arms trapped by it over her head as I captured her mouth. Belle moaned against me, the tip of her tongue lashing across my teeth.

We needed each other. We loved each other. That was all that mattered. We could work through everything, as long as we kept showing up. As long as at the end of the day she held out her hand. As long as every night, I took her to bed. We just had to keep committing.

"I need you in my fucking mouth," I growled, cruising my lips down her neck to dip between the valley of her collarbone. My hand slid behind her, unclasping her bra with one smooth motion to free her swollen breasts. This wasn't like the last time. Belle arched into the contact, offering more of herself with each touch. The message was clear. We were here, and that was all that mattered. I coasted to her nipple, swirling my tongue around its furl until it plumped into a hard pebble, then I nipped it ever so slightly. One tiny drop of milk beaded across it and Belle's eyes widened with sudden embarrassment. Not breaking eye contact, I swiped my tongue along the top of it. Then I licked my lips.

"How many times do I have to tell you?" I rasped. "I want *all of you*. You taste so fucking sweet, beautiful."

I continued down, kissing along the soft skin of her belly. She was softer now, more womanly. My hands sank ever so slightly into the dip of her hips. I didn't think she could be even more of a wet dream, and yet here I was wanting her more tonight than ever before. I hooked my fingers around the waistband of her trousers, drawing them down slowly, allowing my mouth to follow as I revealed more and more of her pale skin. When I reached her knees, I shoved the pants to her ankles, not bothering to remove them either. I didn't have time to find a rope and tie her up, but I needed her at my mercy any way I could get her. I planted my palms on the inside of her thighs and spread her wide open. Brushing my nose along the lace covering her pussy, I breathed in deeply. "This is my favorite scent in the entire world. And you know the best part?"

My eyes drifted up to find her watching me, her neck craned as she bit her lower lip with expectation. There was an almost imperceptible shake of her head.

"It tastes even better," I growled. Shoving the lace to the side, I buried my mouth in her pussy, parting her roughly with my tongue so that I could sweep its tip along the slick heat of her seam. When I reached the swollen knot of her clit, I kissed it softly before tugging it between my teeth.

"Oh my God!" Belle cried.

I pulled back ever so slightly, still close enough that my breath tickled across the engorged flesh. "That's not my name, beautiful."

"Oh my sir!" She moaned, her hips bucking closer to me.

I shifted on to my heels, hooking my arms around her thighs and yanking her pussy to my face. My hands splayed across her stomach pinning her to the edge of the bed as I devoured her. She'd been ready for me. She always was, and seconds later, she unspooled over my tongue, her thighs clamping against the sides of my face. But I didn't stop. I sucked harder, took more, needing to prove that I could push her over the edge as many times as I wanted—as many times as she could take.

Her body writhed against the point where I held her captive to the bed, but I continued the onslaught. She wanted me to be a man. This is what a man did. The only thing he took from a woman was the pride of giving her pleasure. He took her, but only to see the beauty of her unraveling. A real man knew the size of his cock didn't matter nearly as much as what he could do with it—and right now, I was only working with my mouth.

"Please," she panted, but I still didn't stop. "Please, sir, fuck me"

I kept going, enjoying how she begged, knowing she was torn between this pleasure and the other kinds I might give her. I waited until her pleas were nothing more than inaudible moans and groans of pleasure, punctuated by the occasional *sir* or the even rarer *please*. I knew what she wanted, but I could give her more than that. When nothing coming from her made sense anymore, I pushed her onto the bed, her feet still dangling off the edge and stood. Unbuttoning my trousers, I let them fall to my ankles. Stepping forward, I pinned her pants to the floor before reaching down to hoist her thighs around my waist. They popped off at her ankles, leaving her bare save for the scrap of lace still shoved to the side of her pussy. I didn't bother with it. Instead, I lined my dick up until its head was poised at her warm entrance. Belle had dissolved into something primitive, mewling and thrashing with her eyes still closed tightly and her fingers fisting into her sweater.

"Is this what you need, beautiful?" I nudged forward, her soft folds parting around my wide crest. She groaned, desperately circling her hips. "I didn't understand you."

She whimpered, following it with a soft please.

"What?" I repeated, growing painfully aware of the blood rushing to my dick with each second I stayed there, so close to being inside her.

I could see the effort it took her to form the words. As they found their way to her lips, she peeked at me from beneath her long, black lashes. *"Please, sir."*

Fuck. She could have all of me. I plunged into her and she vaulted off the bed from the impact, an unearthly cry rending the air around us. She was so wet, so ready. "You feel fucking amazing, beautiful. I loved feeling you come on my tongue, but now I need to watch you come on my cock. You want it, don't you?"

"Please, give it to me. Please, give it to me...sir," she added breathlessly.

"Take it from me," I grunted. "Let your pussy take what's yours."

Belle splintered at my words, and I felt her contracting over my shaft, urging my climax from me over and over until I unloaded inside her, marking her as my own again. When the last of my pleasure had been drank by her insatiable pussy, I lowered her to the bed and laid down next to her.

"I love you, beautiful," I whispered. "No matter what. Forever."

"Even when I don't deserve it?" she whispered.

"You have all of me. You never have to prove anything to me."

"You've given me everything, and I've—"

"That reminds me," I cut her off before she could say something bad about herself again. Maybe I didn't need to prove her wrong. Maybe I only needed to remind her of the promises we'd made to each other. I sat up and yanked my trousers over my spent cock. Then I walked over to the closet and found her silk robe.

Belle laid on the bed, blinking dreamily at me. "You usually don't want to cover me up so quickly."

"We have company," I reminded her. "If it were up to me, I'd make you walk around here naked all the time."

"Now that would shock Mrs. Winters," she teased, slowly propping herself up on one elbow.

I took her hands and pulled her onto her feet before helping her into the robe. Instead of heading toward the door to the hallway, I walked to the French doors that led to a small balcony we'd ignored until this point. When we first viewed the house, we'd talked about taking our breakfast here in the mornings. But it had hardly been a priority to see to the spot with everything else to be done. We were always too busy to pause and take coffee or watch the sunrise. That needed to change, and we would start changing it tonight. Belle looked curiously at me as I opened the doors and led her outside. I stepped behind her, wrapping my arms around her to protect against the cold, December air. Reaching up, I took her chin and tipped it to the sky. I leaned down, nuzzling my lips against her ear. "I believe I promised you the stars."

Belle gasped as she took in the night. The sky was cloudless, neverending black cloth, punctured by bright spots of light forming constellations over our heads. Here, away from the city and our past, we can see the stars clearly again. We just had to remember to look.

24

BELLE

That night, Penny slept a blissful five straight hours in her bassinet. When she cried out for an early-morning nursing, I rolled over feeling as though I'd turned a page. Smith laid next to me and he stirred when he heard her, opening one bleary eye.

"Need my help?" he asked in a raspy voice that sent shivers dancing through me.

"I've got it," I promised him. I pushed myself up in bed, allowing myself a moment to appreciate how much of him was on display. We had managed to sneak in more lovemaking after Penny fell asleep, and he was still nude, his dick slightly erect and visible under the thin, Egyptian cotton sheet.

Penny's fussing became a more insistent cry, and I tore my eyes away for my husband to go get her. Usually, I carried her to the nursery, and sat there rocking her when she woke at dawn. This morning, I climbed back in bed, cradling her carefully in my arms as I propped myself against the headboard and brought her to nurse.

Smith rolled to his side, watching me without comment. But it was clear something was on his mind.

"Out with it, Price."

"I was just thinking how beautiful you two are. I can't believe we made that." His voice held the familiar note of awe that it always did when he spoke of Penny, and for the first time in as long as I could remember, it filled me with joy. Maybe the medicine was finally working. Maybe things were getting better. Maybe the worst was behind us.

"Oh no," I whispered, realizing that I'd been too distracted last night to think to take it. "I forget to take my pill."

"Does that mean we get another one of these?" He asked with a smirk. "Because I'm game."

"Not that pill," I said dryly. Of course, if things were going in the direction they were last night, I would need to start that back up again sooner rather than later. Smith might be ready for round two, but I needed a little more time.

He mistook my thoughtfulness for something else. "We don't have to have more."

"What?" I asked absently. Then I realized what he meant. "Oh. No, I was thinking about something else. Although, if I'm being honest, I think we should wait a while."

"We'll do whatever you need," he promised. He leaned down to brush a kiss over the downy hair on Penny's head before doing the same to the back of my hand. "I'll go get your medicine."

He jumped out of bed, and I found myself admiring his tight ass as he headed into the bathroom to find it.

"Take your time," I called. "I'm enjoying the view."

When he brought my medication to me, he paused his

hand cupping my chin to direct my eyes to his. He didn't say anything, he just stared before turning away. But I'd seen it there—all the pain, all the uncertainty, all the hope. He'd been with me the whole time. He was as constant as the stars he'd shown me last night. I only had to remember to look and I would find him.

Everything felt new this morning. It had snowed. I discovered Edward downstairs, busily following along as Mrs. Winters barked instructions, and looking more stressed than I'd ever seen him.

"We were trying to beat you out of bed," he said. "I wanted to make you breakfast."

"Are you sure that's a good idea?" I attempted to peek into the bowl he was stirring.

"I won't let him poison you," Mrs. Winters said seriously. Something about her tone suggested she was actually afraid he might do this. He couldn't be that bad of a cook, could he? But just as I thought this, he followed her instruction to crack an egg into the bowl, dropping the yolk, white, *and* the shell.

Nevermind.

"I think I'm going to go for a walk. Smith has Penny," I told them.

"When you come back I'll make you your tea, and you'll have a spot of breakfast," Mrs. Winters said brusquely. I could never be sure if she liked me, but I couldn't doubt that she was taking care of me. And really, what more did I need? Mrs. Winters elbowed Edward. "Why don't you go with her, love? I'll finish this up."

Edward looked gutted to be dismissed from the kitchen

before his coup de grace, but he followed me to the back mud room. Grabbing a spare jacket Smith kept on the hook rather than running upstairs to get his own. We trudged along the back half of the property. There was still so much of the grounds that I hadn't explored yet. I recalled what Dr. Stanton had said about a lake. Or was it a pond? I didn't even know.

"Which way?" Edward asked, his hands buried in his pocket and his shoulders shrugged up towards his ears to protect against the cold.

"Are you sure you want to do this?" I laughed as I realized his nose was already turning red from the chill.

"Are you kidding? I love snow. About the most fun we had as kids was going to Scotland for Christmas. There was always snow and everyone was a little drunk, so we could spend all day playing. I don't know how we all still have our fingers and toes," he confessed.

It was one of the first times he'd spoken so lovingly of his family since he came here. Still, I didn't want to press my luck so I let the conversation naturally segue into other topics, hoping it was a good sign that he hadn't immediately started thinking of his troubled relationship with his brother. Sometimes love took time, I realized. Sometimes it wasn't easy. It was important to remember that the unconditional kind—the type of love everyone wanted—didn't mean flawless. It just meant it was worth it.

"I think there's a shed back around here somewhere or maybe it's a horse barn. I don't know I lost track of all the outbuildings," I admitted to him.

"You've been hanging around my family too long if you can't remember what property you own anymore," he teased.

"I was hugely pregnant when we bought it, and Smith wouldn't allow me to go too far out on the grounds. He was worried I'd overexert myself."

"He didn't seem very worried about that last night, judging from the sound of it."

I gave him a sly grin. "You heard that, huh?"

"They heard that in London, honey," he told me. "I'm just glad you two are working through it."

"I think we have you to thank for that," I said. Edward had come along at just the right time. Maybe it was coincidence, maybe my medication was finally starting to take effect, but I couldn't help but feel lighter with him here. He was a reminder of everything that we'd left behind in London. As long as he was here, everything would be okay.

"You think there's a sled in these stables?" he asked.

"It's worth looking."

But we'd only gotten a few meters away, when Rowan came trudging up from the grounds, a large shovel in his hands.

"Where are you two going?" he asked, coming to a stop.

I hadn't had much contact with the groundskeeper. He spent all of his time outside, which made sense. He seemed respectful of Smith, but not very interested in people. I guess that's why he was good with plants. But I didn't honestly know what all he was working on. I looked at the shovel.

"Just out for a walk," I said. "I heard there was a pond."

"The pond is the other way, ma'am," he said, chewing on each word. "I'm in the middle of a project this way, and I'd thank you to leave it be until I'm finished. It's no place for a lady."

I was temporarily stunned. I opened my mouth, about to

ask him how he dared tell me where to go on my own land when Edward grabbed my hand and tugged me in the other direction

"Let's go find that pond."

Rowan yelled behind us. "That pond may look frozen, but it's not been cold enough. Don't go walking on it!"

"I had no idea he was so bossy," I muttered to Edward, "or rude or sexist."

"That's not what bothered me," Edward said shiftily. "What could he be digging right now in the snow? The ground is frozen. He can't be planting, can he?"

"You're the one with all the estates. I'm sure something has to be planted in winter." I hadn't thought of that. I'd been too busy being offended by the way he'd spoken to me.

"I'm no botanist, but this doesn't seem like the weather for plants," he said pointedly. We walked for another ten minutes without finding the pond Dr. Stanton had spoken of. At that point, Edward's teeth were chattering so loudly that I took pity on him.

"Let's go have a cup of tea," I suggested.

"Yes, your *special tea*," Edward said with emphasis, "and a spot of breakfast. I wouldn't worry about Mrs. Winters. I think you have her wrapped around your finger regardless of how she acts. Remember, we Brits show our love in strange ways."

"Whatever, and it's only special tea because it helps me feed my daughter." I stuck my tongue out at him.

"Well, aren't you fancy?"

"Are you staying for New Year's Eve?" I asked him thoughtfully. Getting through Christmas would be the hardest for him, but New Year's would be a close second.

"Yes, but I plan to get very very drunk," he told me seriously.

"Good."

His eyes narrowed in suspicion at the lack of a lecture. "What are you up to?"

I dashed forward, before he could pepper me with more questions and ducked into the mud room, shrugging off my coat. Edward could get drunk on New Year's. Especially since I planned to invite Tomas. With the baby at home and me nursing, I wouldn't be able to partake in the same festivities, but that didn't mean Edward couldn't have a friend there. Maybe I could even invite Lola. I doubted that Alexander would let Clara make the trek, and she had a baby of her own at home. The thought filled me with sadness for a moment. Of course, she couldn't come. They would be at Balmoral. I was lucky that I had Edward with me now. Next year, I'd have to convince Smith to go to Scotland with the rest of our friends. I suspected our prolonged absence from them had more to do with Smith's concerns about the dangers that surrounded them than the convenience of getting back and forth to London. Seeing Edward had proven to me that wouldn't work. I needed my friends. They were my family. I would just have to show Smith that.

I was already in the kitchen by the time Edward had gotten off his boots and left them by the door.

"Your tea is on the table." Mrs. Winters nodded toward a porcelain teapot, steam rising from its spout, before turning to Edward. "And what will you be having, your highness?"

"Please don't call me that," he said grimly. "I'm just Edward."

I couldn't help wondering if that meant he was questioning his place in the royal family. I shook off my concern. He just needed more time.

I poured myself a hot cup of tea, wrapping my hands around the bone china teacup and relishing how the heat radiated through my frozen fingertips. Breathing in the minty scent, I took a long sip. I hadn't known what to expect from the herbal tea, usually I preferred something stronger myself. A nice Darjeeling, maybe. But I found the Mother's Tea refreshing and floral. I'd been supposed to be taking cups of it a couple of times a day but I kept forgetting. I looked up to Mrs. Winters. "Thank you."

"You need to be having it a couple of times a day according to the box," she said to me. "Although there are other more natural ways to handle—"

"I think this will be enough," I interrupted her. I couldn't imagine that Edward would want to sit through a conversation about breast-feeding.

I finished my first plate of breakfast and stood to make more toast. Mrs. Winters swatted me away, ordering me back to the table so she could do it for me. She was delivering it to me when Smith arrived with Penny in his arms.

"I'm afraid she needs you," he said.

"That's okay," I said, standing to reach for her. But as I did stars appeared on the edges of my vision and I lurched forward, catching myself on the table before I fell. I was dimly aware of concerned cries all around me as I pressed my palm to my temple. I took a moment and straightened up, blinking rapidly. My head felt fuzzy as though I'd had too much to drink. After a moment, it seemed to mostly pass. "I'm okay. I think I stood up too quickly."

Smith hovered next to me protectively, insisting on

carrying Penny into the other room where I could sit and nurse her. He stayed there, watching me like a hawk for further signs of distress, and despite my attempts, I found my eyes growing heavier and heavier.

"Did you get me the wrong medication?" I asked him sleepily.

"I don't think so." He frowned. "I took it out of the bottle marked Sertraline."

"That's the right one," I said slowly. It was getting harder to think. "I just thought maybe you accidentally gave me the sleeping pill."

"Are you tired?" I didn't miss a hint of pride in his voice. "I did keep you rather busy last night."

"That must be it." Truthfully, it probably was. It had been a while since I'd exerted myself so physically.

"Finish up, and take a nap," he said to me.

"But tomorrow is Christmas—" I protested.

"I can handle everything," he said. "You need to rest—" He leaned down to kiss me and whispered "—because I plan on doing a lot of very wicked things to you tonight."

I sighed happily.

"What were you and Edward doing out there anyway?" he asked. "Couldn't wait to play in the snow?"

"That reminds me, he wants to sled. Do you know if the stables may have something like that?" I asked, feeling sleepier and sleepier.

"Stables?" he repeated. "You didn't go all the way out there, did you?"

"No." I yawned. "Rowan stopped me. What is he up to anyway? We were trying to figure out what you plant in winter?"

"Planting? You don't plant anything," he said.

I opened my mouth to tell him about the shovel and the dirt, but found myself too tired to speak.

"Give me the baby, beautiful," he ordered me, "and take your stubborn ass to bed for a while." He saw me all the way up to our room, coming in to tuck me under the covers. Penny squawked a little before settling happily against her daddy's shoulder. I blinked up at him, trying to memorize the moment of seeing my husband with our child, but it was too hard. I was too tired and everything was too fuzzy, so I stopped fighting and let go, knowing that Smith would be right there when I woke up.

25

SMITH

Christmas morning was a leisurely affair. Penny woke us early, and we took our time to gather around the Christmas tree in the sitting room. Edward made coffee that was mostly palatable—as long as I added enough milk to it. Belle contentedly sipped her herbal tea while Penny lay on a blanket staring up at the mesmerizing lights of the Christmas tree. I paused, leaning against the door frame and watched my wife and her best friend, laughing over some inside joke I wasn't privy to. I'd been dreading the holiday, with everything going on, but now, it felt like I'd already been given the only present I wanted: to see her happy.

Belle glanced up, a wide smile carving her face and beckoned me to join them. We opened gifts for minutes or maybe hours. It hardly seemed to matter. Edward had given Belle some fancy shoes she'd scene when they were in London.

"I told you—I have nowhere to wear them," she said, her eyes lingering on them longingly.

Edward shook his head, his curls still tangled from bed.

"Find somewhere to wear them. Life is about making moments not waiting for them."

I made a mental note to find an opportunity to take her out. We might not be able to go as far as London with Penny at home, but once Nora was back in town, we could at least go to this restaurant so that I could meet the famous Tomas that had Belle and Edward giggling behind my back. I wasn't sure if I needed to be jealous of the man or not.

Belle had taken to supplying me with everything a man who owned a country estate might need, from wellies to a new quilted gilet to a truly shocking array of thick, flannel shirts. All I was missing was a hunting dog. I was half-worried I might find a Labrador somewhere under the tree.

"Tired of seeing me in suits, beautiful?"

"I'll never get tired of seeing you in suits," she whispered as I leaned over to kiss her. "But whatever you and Rowan are digging up in the backyard, you probably shouldn't be doing it in a five-thousand-pound, three-piece suit."

I raised an eyebrow. She had a point there. Still, she was digging herself—for information. She'd brought Rowan up a couple of times since yesterday. Thankfully, I could finally tell her what it was.

"There's one more thing I have for you," I told her. "But you have to get dressed first."

"Tell me it comes in Ferrari Red," she purred.

"It's not a car this year," I said, ignoring the way my dick twitched at the thought of her behind a fiery red sports car. Sometimes, Belle seemed to suggest those days were behind us. But I'd be happily fucking her on the top of an Italian sports car's hood when she was ninety. And this year my mind was on our future. And our future wasn't just about her and me or even the baby. We had more to look forward to than the country estate, and it wasn't just about the dreams we shared, but the ones she was building as well.

"I'll watch the baby," Edward offered. Belle dashed upstairs with me right behind her, and we heard him call, "You two better not just be running off to shag!"

She laughed, racing me to get dressed. A few minutes later, she stepped out of her side of the closet dressed in tan leather boots that reached her knees, a thick pair of high waisted pants that hugged her hips with a flannel shirt tucked in to them, showing off her narrow waist. She rolled her eyes when she found me already dressed in jeans and a sweater and pulled a navy Barbour jacket on. I strode closer, tugging it together and buttoning it at the waist.

"I don't want you to get cold," I said.

She stared up at me, like she was looking up at the stars. "You can always warm me up."

"I do believe we were told not to shag." I kissed the tip of her nose, sliding my hand into hers.

Belle wasn't surprised when I led her outside, but she did hesitate. "It's really not a car?"

"I forget how easy you are to please." I couldn't help but smirk. When I first met Belle, I found it stunning when she revealed she loved cars—I knew I'd found my soulmate.

"That's okay," she said huskily. "We have an anniversary coming up."

"Noted." I pulled her toward the grounds.

"Wait," she said as I guided her, "is that what Rowan was up to?"

"Maybe." We walked until we reached a small grove of trees. I paused and drew a blindfold out of my pocket.

She eyed it with interest. "Kinky."

"No shagging, remember?"

"And waste a perfectly good blindfold?" she pouted.

When she put it that way, I made another note: to make sure I knew where it was later. I tied the silk blindfold around her eyes and leaned to murmur in her ear, "Do you trust me?"

"Forever," she said. It was the promise we'd made to each other two years ago. I moved behind her, gripping her waist and slowly leading her past the grove until we reached my Christmas present. When it was in sight, I untied her blindfold. She blinked for a moment, as her eyes readjusted to the daylight.

"You got me a...barn?" She cocked her head, trying to understand. Her eyes skimmed across the once dilapidated building and I saw her beginning to see it was more than that.

Belle hadn't been able to go out on the grounds when we viewed the home. She'd never seen the old stables, but the first time we'd toured Thornham, I'd immediately known what they were meant for. It had taken months and crews coming and going through a back road so as not to draw attention to their presence, but I'd managed to have her Christmas present done in time. When her eyes landed on the reimagined stable doors, she finally saw the sign: Bless.

"Is this...?" She clapped a hand over her mouth, turning to me with tears in her eyes.

"Don't cry, beautiful," I said softly. I'd seen that too many times lately.

"I'm crying because I'm happy. How did you do this?"

"I'll tell you later, but now I want to show you." I grabbed her hand and tugged her toward the new offices of her company. When I opened the arched stable doors, I stepped to the side so she could enter first. Belle's mouth fell open as she entered the large room.

We gutted the place entirely, making it into two large spaces. I took her to the offices first. It was open air, the stable walls plastered over and painted a clean white. We'd kept the beams criss-crossing overhead, their dark, weathered roof a perfect contrast to the modern interior we'd designed below. A polished oak floor had been installed and there were several workstations set up throughout the space. But the centerpiece was a large marble top table with gold cage office chairs for ten around it.

"I'm going to have to hire more people," she said, spinning around to take it all in. She paused when she saw the special spot I'd designed in the corner. Three half walls and a gate surrounded a child's dreamland, complete with stuffed animals and books, a rocking chair, and a crib.

"For Penny," I said, adding, "just in case." I didn't want to pressure my wife to take our daughter to her new offices, but I wanted her to have the option.

"You thought of everything," she said breathlessly.

"Lola helped," I admitted.

Belle snapped her fingers. "That's why she had to come to Briarshead."

"I'm sure she actually wanted to see you, too," I said dryly. I took her hand. "Come on. There's more."

The other half of the space had been made into a sleek warehouse that kept all the unique needs of their clothing rental company in mind. There was a shipping station, organized down to the correct tape for each size box, as well as aisles and aisles of custom-designed racks. Most of the choices here had been Lola's doing.

"I wanted you to be able to work here," I told her. "I know you missed your office in London. It's still there, but—"

She hooked a hand around my neck and shut me up with a kiss. "It's perfect."

"I did okay?" I hadn't gotten a lot right lately. It felt nice to have another win.

"Better than that." She licked her lower lip. "This is what you were up to?"

"Mostly." I shrugged. Christmas didn't seem like the time to bring up the other subjects occupying my mind. "You know, beautiful, you could put on one helluva fashion show here."

"You want me to play dress up for you?"

"It's one of my favorite games," I reminded her. "Do you remember the first time?"

"At Harrods?" She lifted her brow. "A girl doesn't forget a shopping trip like that. Got plans on New Year's?"

"Are we having a party?" I asked.

"I think I could arrange a private viewing of our collection—to start the year out right," she added innocently.

"Naturally." I took a step closer, hooking my index finger in the waistband of her pants. "I'll be honest my favorite item in your office is that big conference table."

"Why's that, Mr. Price?"

"Because, ever since I placed the order, I've been picturing fucking you on it six ways to Sunday."

"Only six ways?" she asked.

I loved it when she challenged me. I scooped her off her feet, our mouths colliding together, as I carried her back into the office. When we reached the conference table, I lowered her to the ground.

"We need to hurry," she said, panting, as she fumbled to unbuckle my jeans.

There would be time later to explore all the spectacular potential of the table's smooth marble top. For now, I had to agree. Christmas was only just beginning. I spun her away from me and yanked her pants down, bending her over the table.

I ran a finger down her ass. "It's been a long time since I fucked you like this, beautiful. Next time..." I pressed my thumb against the tight pink pucker and she groaned, her hands splaying as she trembled.

Pulling my cock free, I pressed it against her slick seam until it popped past her tight folds and found its home. My thumb pressed farther as I pistoned inside her, and she cried out.

"Who does this pussy belong to?" I demanded.

"You, sir."

"And this ass?"

"You, sir."

I caught her hair with my free hand and yanked her up, kissing her roughly as I continued to fuck her with my finger inside her tight ass. My lips coasted to her jawline over to her ear. "And who do you belong to, beautiful?"

"You, sir. Forever," she whispered. "All of me belongs to you."

Her words released me and I groaned as I spilled inside her. She clenched around my dick and my thumb, her whole body shaking as she came. I wrapped an arm around her waist, holding her against me until we'd both gone completely still.

"I love you," I murmured. "I don't want to let you go."

She twisted her neck, her hair still tangled in my fist. Her eyes were bright and so alive. "Then don't."

BELLE

Something was wrong. I knew it the first time I tried to nurse Penny the day after Christmas. I remembered what the nurse at the clinic had said. She was right. Overnight my happy two month-old had become a tyrant. Every time I put her to the breast, she screamed. Smith took turns with me, trying to calm her. The magic of the season seemed to be officially over.

"Can you give her a bottle?" Edward suggested gently after two hours of nonstop screaming.

"I'll have to pump." I heaved myself up from the chair I'd collapsed into after Smith had taken for his turn at attempting to calm our little beast. It took me a few minutes to find it. I hadn't even unpacked it, since I'd never needed to give her a bottle. With Edward's help, I managed to get it up and running. But half an hour later, barely anything had come out.

Smith appeared in the door of the nursery, Penny sobbing in his arms. She was hungry, and I couldn't feed her. After everything I'd done, it hadn't been enough.

"I think my milk is gone," I said in a hollow voice. I didn't understand. Doctor Stanton had told me to feed her more and drink the tea. I was due to go in for a follow-up weight check this week, but I already knew that he would tell me. "She needs formula."

Smith walked over and placed a strong hand on my shoulder. "I'm sorry, beautiful. Why don't I run to town and get some? Maybe you need to drink more of that tea?"

I shrugged, swallowing hard. Terrible thoughts screamed in my head drowning out Penny's wails. Every time I was happy—even for a moment—I was punished. This was my fault. I'd been distracted. I'd spent too much time away from the baby. I hadn't drank enough of the sodding tea. I wasn't enough. No matter how hard I tried.

"My turn," Edward held out his hands. "Go take a minute. She'll be fine."

But she wouldn't be. Not until Smith returned with food. It was her most basic need and I couldn't provide it. I walked out of the room not really knowing where I was going. I'd woken to feed Penny and this had started. We were all still in robes and pajamas. Smith followed me in and changed.

"Are you going to be okay?" he asked, giving me a worried look. "Maybe you should come with me."

I shook my head. "I'm going to take a shower, grab my medication, and get cleaned up."

"I won't be gone long," he promised.

He kissed me goodbye and I retreated to the comfort of my monotonous routine. At least, I still knew how to wash my hair and get dressed. When I emerged from the shower, I wiped steam from the mirror. Yesterday, I was sure I saw myself there staring back at me. Today, she seemed like a stranger. What was happening to me? I picked up the pill bottle, checking the label so I didn't grab the wrong one. Part of me was tempted to take a sleeping pill anyway and claim it was an accident. I could wake up tomorrow and this would be over, but that wasn't going to help me or my baby.

Smith was right. We would get through this. A shrill scream punctuated the air and I closed my eyes before I left to do what I could to soothe my daughter, knowing it would never be enough.

SMITH

The pharmacy was just opening when I pulled the Range Rover into the parking spot in front. I'd paused long enough at home to grab the tea Belle had been drinking. It was a longshot, but I'd seen the heartbreak on her face when she couldn't nurse Penny. She'd come so far in the last few weeks. I wouldn't let her give up without a fight. Not when she was so close to finding herself again. We could do more. I could do more.

A bell tinkled as I opened the door and stepped inside. Behind the far counter, a woman looked up in surprise from the register.

"Early start," she said by way of greeting.

"Baby formula," I said, looking around. "It's a bit of an emergency actually."

She circled the counter quickly, leading me to the small cache of infant supplies in the shop. "What kind?"

"I have no idea." I'd never felt so helpless. Penny's screams were still ringing in my ears. I could only think of bringing her what she needed. "My wife was nursing her, but there was no milk this morning. She won't stop screaming."

"In that case." She piled a few canisters into her arms. "We can troubleshoot later, but let's get you home." She carried them to the counter and began ringing them up, peppering me with questions as she did. "Did she try pumping?"

"Yes. This morning," I said, feeling another wave of frustration.

"Did her period start up again? That can affect some women," she said.

"I don't think so. Our daughter is only two months old."

"There are some herbs she can try. Give the baby a bottle but have her keep putting her to the breast to feed," she advised. "She should keep pumping and take warm showers."

I made mental notes as she rattled off suggestion after suggestion. I gave her a grateful smile as she handed me a bag. I'd turned to leave when I remembered the herbs.

"The herbs?" I said. I yanked the tin of tea out of my pocket. "She was taking this. Should she try something else, too?"

She picked up the tin and pried off the lip, lowering her nose to sniff it. Her eyes widened in surprise. "This is what she's been drinking?"

"Yes, I think she got it here." I cursed myself for not paying more attention.

"Mint. Sage." She sniffed again. "Nettle. This would dry up her milk supply. We usually give it to mothers who want to wean...or mothers who've lost..." She trailed off, shaking her head. "There must have been a mistake. Maybe she asked for the wrong one."

I closed my eyes. "She's been drinking it constantly. The doctor told her the baby needed to gain weight."

"Have her do all the things I told you." She pulled another tin out. "She should drink this one. It will taste a bit like licorice. That's the one she wants, if she still wants to nurse."

"Thank you," I called, grabbing the tea tin. The Range Rover's wheels spun on the frost still covering the streets as I hauled ass back toward Thornham. It had all been a stupid mistake, and she was paying the price for it. I wouldn't let her feel guilty. Maybe something could be done, if she wanted. I'd just passed the village entrance when the speakers rang with an incoming call. I punched accept.

"Now's not a good time."

"Where are you?" Georgia's harsh voice cut in. "You sound like you're driving."

"I had to run to the village." I didn't bother to fill her in on the particulars. I doubted she would care.

"I'm on my way to you," she said.

"Christmas was yesterday," I said dryly.

"Funny," she said, not sounding the least bit amused. We'd never been the caroling around the piano types, so I doubted her sudden visit had anything to do with the holidays.

I turned down the country lane at the Thornham sign, the road instantly becoming a bumpy, dirt path. "What's going on?"

"Well, first, tell your wife to call her best friend back before Clara has a stroke."

"Is something wrong?"

"She's been trying to reach her for weeks, and I had to

stop Clara from getting in the car and driving from Scotland to Sussex. She's worried about her."

"Tell her Edward's with her," I said. "That should calm her down."

"Probably," Georgia admitted.

"Why are you coming?" I asked as Thornham came into view.

"It's about your house," she said grimly. "I got the file. I think you could use someone there to help you look into this locally."

A chill raced across the back of my neck like a single icy finger had pressed against it. "What did you find?"

"We'll figure it out. See you tonight." She hung up before I could get any real answers from her.

Georgia had seen the closed report—the one Longborn hadn't wanted to give her. Now Georgia was on her way to Briarshead. That wasn't a good sign. I was trying to decide how to tell Belle that we'd have another visitor when I pulled up to the house and saw the front door open.

I threw on the SUV's parking brake, grabbed my shopping bag, and raced up the front steps in a panic. I couldn't deny it any longer. This was about more than Belle or me. There was something about Thornham that wasn't right. I wasn't a man who believed in ghosts. Not the kind you found in darkened hallways, at least. I knew well enough of the ghosts we all carried in our memories. But nothing had been right since we moved here.

When I reached the open door, I ran directly into Nora, who dropped the cup she was holding in surprise.

"I'm sorry," I bit out as she bent to pick it up.

"I just got here," she said. "I went up to check on Belle." She gathered the pieces into her palm.

"Is she okay? She had a rough morning with Penny." I didn't have time to fill her in on more particulars. Georgia was on her way. The baby needed to be fed. And in the last few hours, my life had begun to crash down around me.

"She's not in her room." Nora shrugged. "She probably went for a walk. Where's the baby?"

"Edward has her in the nursery," I told her. I passed her the bag. "I have no idea how to make one of these. Can you?"

She peeked inside to find the formula and a few bottles the pharmacist had sent along. "Of course."

She hurried off, and I was grateful not to waste more time with questions. I climbed the stairs, preparing myself to relay all the information that has been dumped on me in the last half hour. Stepping into the nursery, I found it empty.

I backed up, looking around. I took a few steps down the hall and banged on Edward's door. He opened it, a towel wrapped around his waist.

"Where's Penny?" I asked, but I didn't wait for an answer.

"What's going on?" he yelled. "She fell asleep. Belle came in and took her to lie down."

I raced back to the nursery, my eyes landing on an empty crib. I already knew what I'd find when I went to the master bedroom. An empty bed. An empty bassinet.

Edward was still yelling when I rushed down the stairs. I flew past Nora, who came running after me with a bottle. Rowan appeared coming from the direction of Belle's new offices, carrying a bag of sod over his shoulders. He'd stubbornly insisted on working on the landscaping around it even mid-winter.

"You look like the devil's after you," he called.

"Have you seen my wife?"

"Not this morning. I just came from the stables…"

His words stole the last hope I had. I ran in the opposite direction. Belle didn't know the grounds like I did, but somehow—and I couldn't explain it—I knew exactly where she was.

The pond sat almost a kilometer away from the main house. I was vaguely aware of others coming behind me. When the pond finally came into sight, I hesitated only a moment before sprinting forward. She was there, her back turned to me, blonde hair whipping in the wind. I was a few meters away when I realized she wasn't standing on its bank.

"Belle," I called, scared I would startle her, scared she would walk farther onto the ice. "Beautiful!"

Penny's screams carried through the air, and fear seized me. I'd never known fear until that moment, watching my world on that thin sheet of ice. Belle finally turned and I beckoned her closer. "Beautiful, come to me."

Her eyes were hollow again—a ghost's eyes—then she blinked, startling with confusion.

"Careful," I warned. "Just walk towards me."

Her eyes flickered in fear to the ice below her and she tightened her grip on Penny. "Smith? Where…?"

I couldn't risk stepping on to the ice to bring her back to safety. She had to come to me, but she didn't move. Behind us, there were distant shouts. Our eyes locked on each other and everything else faded away.

"Forever, beautiful," I reminded her, my promise becoming entreaty.

Please God, don't take my forever. Don't take my heart. Don't take my world.

"Please," I begged her, holding out my hand. "Please come back to me."

There was no command in my voice. I wasn't ordering her. I was begging for my life out there on that barely frozen pond.

Belle slid her foot forward, her chest heaving as the next followed. Her eyes stayed trained on me, and I urged her forward with my hand extended. Time slowed until there was only her and me and our heartbeats. Her fingers closed over mine and time shot forward. Penny's cries flooded the air along with shouts and a terrible splintering pop below our feet. I grasped her wrist, wrenching her off the ice, away from danger, back to me. She crashed into my arms, a thunderclap booming behind us as the ice gave way where she'd just stood.

"Smith," she sobbed my name, clutching me, Penny pressed between us wailing. "Smith..."

I looked into her wide eyes and found the fear pounding inside me there.

"Help me," she pleaded. "I don't know...why..."

The ice collapsed behind us, sending the water trapped below cresting over the splintered pieces until there was hardly any of it left. I pressed her closer, whispering promises as I kissed the top of her head followed by Penny's. They were safe, and nothing like this would hapen again. I wouldn't allow it. I never thought it would come to this.

But I would protect her from anything—even herself.

ABOUT THE AUTHOR

GENEVA LEE is the *New York Times*, *USA Today*, and internationally bestselling author of over a dozen novels, including the Royals Saga which has sold two million copies worldwide. She lives in Washington state with her husband and three children, and she co-owns Away With Words Bookshop with her sister.

Geneva is married to her high school sweetheart. He's always the first person to read her books. Sometimes, he reads as she writes them. Last year, they were surprised by finding out Geneva was pregnant with their third child. They welcomed a beautiful baby girl in 2020.

When she isn't working or writing, Geneva likes to read, bake ridiculous cakes, and watch television. She loves to travel and is always anxious to go on a new adventure.

Printed in Great Britain
by Amazon